An Encroaching Shadow

"How about the man in your bed, Betty?" I said. "May I see him?"

She shrugged and waved her hand at a door. "Right through there. He's still out cold."

I nodded and set the glass down on a table that had a coaster on it. I went through the door and looked at the man in the bed. It was a big, fancy bed, oval in shape, and it made the man look smaller than he was. I hadn't seen him in more than a year and there were some new lines in his face and more grey in his hair than I remembered. His name was Michael Padillo and he spoke six or seven languages without accent, was handy with either a gun or a knife, and could make what has been called the best whiskey sour in Europe.

His other chief distinction was that a lot of people thought he was dead. A lot more hoped that he was.

CAST A YELLOW SHADOW

Also by Ross Thomas

The Singapore Wink
The Fools in Town Are on My Side

Forthcoming from
MYSTERIOUS PRESS

CAST A YELLOW SHADOW

ROSS THOMAS

THE MYSTERIOUS PRESS · New York

MYSTERIOUS PRESS EDITION

This Mysterious Press Edition is published by arrangement with
William Morrow & Co., Inc., 105 Madison Avenue, New York,
New York 10016.

Cover design by George Corsillo

Mysterious Press books are published in association with
Warner Books, Inc.
666 Fifth Avenue
New York, N.Y. 10103

W A Warner Communications Company

Printed in the United States of America

First Mysterious Press Printing: February, 1987

10 9 8 7 6 5 4 3

To J. Edwin and Laura E.

— ONE —

T he call came while I was trying to persuade a lameduck Congressman to settle his tab before he burned his American Express card. The tab was $18.35 and the Congressman was drunk and had already made a pyre of the cards he held from Carte Blanche, Standard Oil, and the Diner's Club. He had used a lot of matches as he sat there at the bar drinking Scotch and burning the cards in an ashtray. "Two votes a precinct," he said for the dozenth time. "Just two lousy votes a precinct."

"When they make you an ambassador, you'll need all the credit you can get," I said as Karl handed me the phone. The Congressman thought about that for a moment, frowned and shook his head, said something more about two votes a precinct, and set fire to the American Express card. I said hello into the phone.

"McCorkle?" It was a man's voice.

"Yes."

"This is Hardman." It was a soft bass voice with a lot

1

of bulldog gravy and grits in it. Hardman, the way he said it, was two distinct words, an adjective and a noun, and both got equal billing.

"What can I do for you?"

"Make me a reservation for lunch tomorrow? Bout one-fifteen?"

"You don't need a reservation."

"Just socializin a little."

"I'm off the ponies," I said. "I haven't made a bet in two days."

"That's what they been tellin me. Man, you trying to quit winner?"

"Just trying to quit. What's on your mind?"

"Well, I got me a little business over in Baltimore." He paused. I waited. I prepared for a long wait. Hardman was from Alabama or Mississippi or Georgia or one of those states where they all talk alike and where it takes a long weekend to get to the point.

"You've got business in Baltimore and you want a reservation for one-fifteen tomorrow and you want to know why I haven't made book with you in two days. What else?"

"Well, we was supposed to pick somethin up off a boat over there in Baltimore and there was a little trouble and this white boy got hurt. So Mush—you know Mush?"

I told him I knew Mush.

"So Mush was bout to get hisself hurt by a couple of mothers when this white boy steps in and sort of helps Mush out—know what I mean?"

"Perfectly."

"Say wha?"

"Go on."

"Well, one of these cats had a blade and he cuts the

white boy a little, but not fore he'd stepped in and helped out for Mush—know what I mean?"

"Why call me?"

"Well, Mush brings the white boy back to Washington cause he's hit his head and bleedin and passed out and all."

"And you need some blood tonight?"

Hardman chuckled and it seemed to rumble over the phone. "Shit, baby, you somethin!"

"Why me?"

"Well, this boy got nothin on him. No money—"

"Mush checked that out, I'd say."

"No gold, no ID, no billfold, nothin. Just a little old scrap of paper with your address on it."

"Has he got a description, or do all white folks look alike?"

"Bout five-eleven," Hardman said, "maybe even six feet. Maybe. Short hair, little grey in it. Dark for an ofay. Looks like he been out in the sun a whole lot. Bout your age, only skinnier, but then, hell, who ain't?"

I tried to make nothing out of my voice; no tone, no interest. "Where do you have him?"

"Where I'm at, pad over on Fairmont." He gave me the address. "Figure you know him? He's out cold."

"I might," I said. "I'll be over. You get a doctor?"

"Done come and gone."

"I'll be there as soon as I can catch a cab."

"You won't forget about that reservation?"

"It's taken care of." I hung up.

Karl, the bartender I had imported from Germany, was deep in conversation with the Congressman. I signaled him to come down to the other end of the bar.

"Take care of the Right Honorable," I said. "Call him

a cab—the company that specializes in drunks. If he doesn't have any money, have him sign a tab and we'll send him a bill."

"He's got a committee hearing tomorrow at nine in the Rayburn Building," Karl said. "It's on reforestation. It's about the redwoods. I was planning on going anyhow so I'll pick him up in the morning and make sure he gets there."

Some people hang around police stations. Karl hung around Congress. He had been in the States for less than a year but he could recite the names of the one hundred Senators and the four hundred and thirty-five Representatives in alphabetical order. He knew how they voted on every roll call. He knew when and where committees met and whether their sessions were open or closed. He could tell you the status of any major piece of legislation in either the Senate or the House and make you a ninety to ninety-five per cent accurate prediction on its chance for passage. He read the Congressional Record faithfully and snickered while he did it. He had worked for me before in a saloon I had once owned in Bonn, but the Bundestag had never amused him. He found Congress one long laugh.

"Just so he gets home," I said, "although he looks as if he'll fade before closing." The Congressman was drooping a bit over his glass.

Karl gave him a judicious glance. "He's good for two more and then I'll get him some coffee. He'll make it."

I told him to close up, nodded good night to a handful of regular customers and a couple of waiters, walked east to Connecticut Avenue and turned right towards the Mayflower Hotel. There was one cab at the hotel stand and I climbed into its back seat and gave the driver the address. He turned to look at me.

4

"I don't ever go over there after midnight," he said.

"Don't tell me. Tell the hack inspector."

"My life's worth more'n eighty cents."

"We'll make it an even dollar."

I got a lecture on why George Wallace should be President on the way to the Fairmont Street address. It was an apartment building, fairly new, flanked by forty- or fifty-year-old row houses. I paid the driver and told him he needn't wait. He snorted, quickly locked all the doors, and sped off. Inside I found the apartment number and rang the bell. I could hear chimes inside. Hardman answered the door.

"Come in this house," he said.

I went in. A voice from somewhere, a woman's voice, yelled: "You tell him to take off his shoes, hear?"

I looked down. I was standing on a deep pile carpet that was pure white.

"She don't want her white rug messed up," Hardman said and indicated his own shoeless feet. I knelt down and took off my shoes. When I rose Hardman handed me a drink.

"Scotch-and-water O.K.?"

"Fine." I looked around the livingroom. It was L-shaped and had an orange couch and some teak and leather chairs, a dining table, also of teak, and a lot of brightly colored pillows that were carefully scattered here and there to make it all look casual. There were some loud prints on the wall. A lot of thought seemed to have gone into the room, and the total effect came off fairly well and just escaped being flashy.

A tall brown girl in red slacks swayed into the room shaking down a thermometer. "You know Betty?" Hardman asked.

5

I said no. "Hello, Betty."

"You're McCorkle." I nodded "That man's sick," she said, "and there ain't no use trying to talk to him now. He's out for another hour. That's what Doctor Lambert say. And he also say he can be moved all right when he wakes up. So if he's a friend of yours, would you kindly move him when he does wake up? He's got my bed and I don't plan sleeping on no couch. That's where Hard's going to sleep."

"Now, honey—"

"Don't honey me, you no good son-of-a-bitch." She didn't raise her voice when she said it. She didn't have to. "You bring in some cut-up drunk and dump him into my bed. Whyn't you take him to the hospital? Or to your house, 'cept that fancy wife of yours wouldn't have stood for it." Betty turned to me, and waved a hand at Hardman. "Look at him. Six-feet, four-inches tall, dresses just so fine, goes around pronouncing his name 'Hard-Man,' and then lets some little five-foot-tall tight twat lead him around by the nose. Get me a drink." Betty collapsed on the couch and Hardman hastily mixed her a drink.

"How about the man in your bed, Betty?" I said. "May I see him?"

She shrugged and waved her hand at a door. "Right through there. He's still out cold."

I nodded and set the glass down on a table that had a coaster on it. I went through the door and looked at the man in the bed. It was a big, fancy bed, oval in shape, and it made the man look smaller than he was. I hadn't seen him in more than a year and there were some new lines in his face and more grey in his hair than I remembered. His name was Michael Padillo and he spoke six or seven languages without accent, was handy with either a gun or a knife, and could make what has been called the best whiskey sour in Europe.

His other chief distinction was that a lot of people thought he was dead. A lot more hoped that he was.

— TWO —

The last time I had seen Michael Padillo he had been falling off a barge into the Rhine. There had been a fight with guns and fists and a broken bottle. Padillo and a Chinese called Jimmy Ku had gone over the side. Somebody had been aiming a shotgun at me at the time and the shotgun had gone off, so I was never sure whether Padillo had drowned or not until I received a postcard from him. It had been mailed from Dahomey in West Africa, contained a one-word message—"Well"—and had been signed with a "P." He had never been much of one to write.

On dull days after the postcard came I sometimes sat around and drank too much and speculated about how Padillo had made it from the Rhine to the West Coast of Africa and whether he liked the climate. He was good at getting from one place to another. When he was not helping to run the saloon that we owned in Bonn he had been on call to one of those spooky government agencies that kept sending him to such places as Lodz and Leipzig and Tollin. I never asked what he did; he never told me.

When his agency decided to trade him for a couple of defectors to the East, Padillo tried to buy up his contract. He succeeded that spring night when he fell off the barge into the Rhine about a half-mile up river from the American Embassy. His agency wrote him off and no one from the Embassy ever came around to inquire about what happened to the nice man who used to own half of Mac's Place in Bad Godesberg.

Padillo's attempt to retire from the secret-agent dodge had involved both of us in a trip to East Berlin and back. During our absence somebody had blown up the saloon in revenge for some real or imagined slight so I collected the insurance money, got married, and opened Mac's Place in Washington a few blocks up from K Street, west of Connecticut Avenue. It's dark and it's quiet and the prices discourage the annual pilgrimages of high school graduating classes.

I stood there in the bedroom and looked at Padillo for a while. I couldn't see where he had been cut. The covers were up to his neck. He lay perfectly still in the bed, breathing through his nose. I turned and went back into the livingroom with the white carpet.

"How bad is he hurt?" I asked Hardman.

"Got him in the ribs and he bled some. Mush say that boy damn near got both those cats. Moved nice and easy and quick, just like he'd been doin it all his life."

"He's no virgin," I said.

"Friend of yours?"

"My partner."

"What you gonna do with him?" Betty said.

"He's got a small suite in the Mayflower; I'll move him

there when he wakes up and get somebody to stay with him."

"Mush'll stay," Hardman said. "Mush owes him a little."

"Doctor Lambert say he wasn't hurt bad, but that he's all tired out—exhaustion," Betty said. She looked at her watch. It had a lot of diamonds on it. "He'll be waking up in bout half an hour."

"I take it Doctor Lambert didn't call the cops," I said.

Hardman sniffed. "Now what kind of fool question is that?"

I should have known. "May I use your phone?"

Betty pointed it out. I dialed a number and it rang for a long time. Nobody answered. The phone was the push-button kind so I tried again on the chance that I had misdialed or mispunched. I was calling my wife and I was having a husband's normal reactions when his wife fails to answer the telephone at one-forty-five in the morning. I let it ring nine times and then hung up.

My wife was a correspondent for a Frankfurt paper, the one with the thoughtful editorials. It was her second assignment in the States. I had met her in Bonn and she knew about Padillo and the odd jobs he had once done for the quietly inefficient rival of the CIA. My wife's name was Fredl and before she married me it was Fraulein Doktor Fredl Arndt. The Doktor had been earned in Political Science at the University of Bonn and some of her tony friends addressed me as Herr Doktor McCorkle, which I bore well enough. After a little more than a year of marriage I found myself very much in love with my wife. I even liked her.

I called the saloon and got Karl. "Has my wife called?"

"Not tonight."

"The Congressman still there?"

"He's closing up the place with coffee and brandy. The tab is now $24.85 and he's still looking for two votes a precinct. If he had had them, he could have made the runoff."

"Maybe you can help him look. If my wife calls, tell her I'll be home shortly."

"Where're you at?"

"Right before the at," I said. Karl had no German accent, but he had learned his English from the endless procession of Pfc's who came out of the huge Frankfurt PX during the postwar years. As a seven-year-old orphan, he had bought their cigarettes to sell on the black market.

"Never end a sentence with a preposition," he recited.

"Not never; just seldom. I'm at a friend's. I have to run an errand so if Fredl calls, tell her I'll be home shortly."

"See you tomorrow."

"Right."

Hardman raised his six feet, four inches of large bone and hard muscle from a chair, skirted around Betty as if she would bite, and walked over to mix another drink. He was as close to a racketeer as Washington had to offer, I suppose. He was far up in the Negro numbers hierarchy, ran a thriving bookie operation, and had a crew of boosters out lifting whatever they fancied from the city's better department stores and specialty shops. He wore three- or four-hundred-dollar suits and eighty-five-dollar shoes and drove around town in a bronze Cadillac convertible talking to friends and acquaintances over his radio-telephone. He was a folk hero to the Negro youth in Washington and the police let him alone most of the time because he wasn't too greedy and paid his dues where it counted.

Oddly enough I had met him through Fredl, who had

once done a feature on Negro society in Washington. Hardman ranked high in one clique of that mysteriously stratified social realm. After the story appeared in the Frankfurt paper, Fredl sent him a copy. The story was in German, but Hardman had had it translated and then dropped around the saloon carrying a couple of dozen long-stemmed roses for my wife. He had been a regular customer since and I patronized his bookie operation. Hardman liked to show the translation of the feature to friends and point out that he should be regarded as a celebrity of international note.

Holding three drinks in one giant hand, he moved over to Betty and served her and then handed one to me.

"Did my partner come off a ship?" I asked.

"Uh-huh."

"Which one?"

"Flyin a Liberian flag and believe it or not was out of Monrovia. She's called the *Frances Jane* and was carryin cocoa mostly."

"Mush wasn't picking up a pound of cocoa."

"Well, it was a little more'n a pound."

"How'd it happen?"

"Mush was waitin to meet somebody off that boat and was just hangin around waitin for him when the two of them jumped him. Next thing he knows he's lyin down and this friend of yours has done stepped in and was mixin with both of them. He doin fine till they start with the knives. One of them gets your friend in the ribs and by then Mush is back up and saps one of them and then they both take off. Your friend's down and out so Mush goes through his pockets and comes up with your address and calls me. I tell him to hang around to see if he can make his meet and if he don't connect in ten minutes, to come back to Washington and bring the white boy with him. He bled some on Mush's car."

"Tell him to send me a bill."

"Shit, man, I didn't mean it like that."

"I didn't think you did."

"Mush'll be back in a little while. He'll take you and your buddy down to the hotel."

"Fine."

I got up and walked back into the bedroom. Padillo was still lying quietly in the bed. I stood there looking at him, holding my drink and smoking a cigarette. He stirred and opened his eyes. He saw me, nodded carefully, and then moved his eyes around the room.

"Nice bed," he said.

"Have a good nap?"

"Pleasant. How bad am I?"

"You'll be O.K. Where've you been?"

He smiled slightly, licked his lips, and sighed. "Out of town," he said.

Hardman and I helped Padillo to dress. He had a white shirt that had been washed but not ironed, a pair of Khaki pants in the same condition, a Navy pea jacket, and black shoes with white cotton socks.

"Who's your new tailor?" I asked.

Padillo glanced down at his clothes. "Little informal, huh?"

"Betty washed em out in her machine," Hardman said. "Blood hadn't dried too much, so it came out easy. Didn't get a chance to iron em."

"Who's Betty?"

"You've been sleeping in her bed," I said.

"Thank her for me."

13

"She's in the next room. You can thank her yourself."

"Can you walk?" Hardman said.

"Is there a drink in the next room along with Betty?"

"Sure."

"I can walk."

He could, although he moved slowly. I carried the forbidden shoes. Padillo paused at the door and put one hand on the jamb to brace himself. Then he walked on into the livingroom. "Thanks for the use of your bed, Betty," he said to the tall brown girl.

"You're welcome. How you feel?"

"A little rocky, but I think it's mostly dope. Who bandaged me?"

"Doctor."

"He give me a shot?"

"Uh-huh. Should be bout worn off."

"Just about is."

"Man wants a drink," Hardman said. "What you like?"

"Scotch, if you have it," Padillo said.

Hardman poured a generous drink and handed it to Padillo. "How's yours, Mac?"

"It's okay."

"Mush'll be here any minute," Hardman said. "He'll take you down to the hotel."

"Where am I staying?" Padillo asked.

"At your suite in the Mayflower."

"My suite?"

"I booked it in your name and it's paid for monthly out of your share of the profits. It's small—but quietly elegant. You can take it off your income tax if you ever get around to filing it."

"How's Fredl?"

"We got married."

14

"You're lucky."

Hardman looked at his watch. "Mush'll be here any minute," he said again.

"Thanks for all your help—yours and Betty's," Padillo said.

Hardman waved a big hand. "You saved us having a big razzoo in Baltimore. What you mess in that for?"

Padillo shook his head slowly. "I didn't see your friend. I just turned a corner and there they were. I thought they were after me. Whichever one had the knife knew how to use it."

"You off that boat?" Hardman said.

"Which one?"

"The *Frances Jane*."

"I was a passenger."

"Didn't run across a little old Englishman, name of Landeed, about fifty or fifty-five, with crossed eyes?"

"I remember him."

"He get off the boat?"

"Not in Baltimore," Padillo said. "His appendix burst four days out of Monrovia. They stored him away in the ship's freezer."

Hardman frowned and swore. He put heart into it. The chimes rang and Betty went to open the door and admitted a tall Negro dressed in a crow-black suit, white shirt, and dark maroon tie. He wore sunglasses at two-thirty in the morning.

"Hello, Mush," I said.

He nodded at me and the nod took in Betty and Hardman. He crossed over to Padillo. "How you feeling?" His voice was precise and soft.

"Fine," Padillo said.

"This is Mustapha Ali," Hardman told Padillo. "He's

15

the cat that brought you down from Baltimore. He's a Black Muslim, but you can call him Mush. Everybody else does."

Padillo looked at Mush. "Are you really a Muslim?"

"I am," the man said gravely.

Padillo said something in Arabic. Mush looked surprised, but responded quickly in the same language. He seemed pleased.

"What are you talkin, Mush?" Hardman asked.

"Arabic."

"Where you learn Arabic?"

"Records, man, records. I'll need it when I get to Mecca."

"You the goddamndest cat I ever seen," Hardman said.

"Where'd you learn Arabic?" Mush asked Padillo.

"From a friend."

"You speak it real good."

"I've had some practice lately."

"We'd better get you to the hotel," I told Padillo. He nodded and stood up slowly.

"Thanks very much for all your help," he said to Betty. She said it was nothing and Hardman said he would see me tomorrow at lunch. I nodded, thanked Betty, and followed Padillo out to Mush's car. It was a new Buick, a big one, and had a telephone in the front and a five-inch Sony television in the back.

"I want to stop by my place on the way to the hotel," I said to Mush. "It won't take long."

He nodded and we drove in silence. Padillo stared out the window. "Washington's changed," he said once. "What happened to the streetcars?"

"Took em off in 'sixty-one," Mush said.

Fredl and I lived in one of those new brick and glass

16

apartments that have blossomed just south of Dupont Circle in a neighborhood that once was made up of three- and four-story rooming houses that catered to students, waiters, car washers, pensioners, and professional tire changers. Speculators tore down the rooming houses, covered the ground with asphalt, and called them parking lots for a while. When enough parking lots were put together, the speculators would apply for a government-insured loan, build an apartment house, and call it The Melanie or The Daphne after a wife or a girl friend. The rents for a two-bedroom apartment in those places were based on the supposition that both husband and wife were not only richly employed, but lucky in the stockmarket.

Nobody ever seemed to care what had happened to the students, waiters, car washers, pensioners and the professional tire changers.

Mush parked the car in the circular driveway where it said no parking and we rode the elevator up to the eighth floor.

"Fredl will be glad to see you," I told Padillo. "She might even invite you to dinner." I opened the door. The light from one large lamp burned in the livingroom, but the lamp had been knocked to the floor and the shade was lying a foot or so away. I went over and picked up the lamp, put it on the table, and replaced the shade. I looked in the bedrooms, but that seemed a foolish thing to do. She wasn't there. I walked back into the livingroom and Padillo was standing near the record player, holding a piece of paper in his right hand. Mush stood by the door.

"A note," I said.

"A note," he agreed.

"But not from Fredl."

"No. It's from whoever took her away."

"A ransom note," I said. I didn't want to read it.

"Sort of."

"How much do they want?"

Padillo saw that I didn't want to read the note. He put it down on the coffee table.

"Not much," he said. "Just me."

— THREE —

I sat down in my favorite chair and looked at the carpet. Then I watched Padillo turn to Mush and say: "You may as well go on back. This will take a while." I looked at Mush. He nodded his head. "Anything you want me to do?" he asked. He sounded interested.

"Nothing right now," Padillo said.

He nodded his head again. "You know where to get in touch."

"I know," Padillo said.

Mush turned quickly and left. He closed the door and the lock barely made a noise as it clicked into place. I looked around the livingroom. The pictures were still on the walls, some that Fredl had brought from Germany, some I had brought, and some that we had decided on together in Washington and New York. The books were still in the bookcase that covered one wall. The furniture, an odd assortment, but comfortable, was still in place. Only a lamp had been upset. I liked the room. It had a

19

couple of personalities in it. There was a small bar in one corner that was a facet of one of those personalities. I got up and walked over to it.

"Scotch?" I asked Padillo.

"Scotch."

"What's the note say?"

"You'd better read it."

"All right. I'll read it."

I handed him the Scotch. He picked up the note and handed it to me. It was typed, single-spaced, undated, and unsigned.

Dear Mr. McCorkle:

We have taken Mrs. McCorkle into our custody. By this time you will have heard from your colleague, Mr. Michael Padillo, who was due to arrive in Baltimore this evening aboard the *Frances Jane*. When Mr. Padillo has performed the assignment which we have requested of him, we shall release Mrs. McCorkle quite unharmed.

We must caution you, however, not to inform the police or the Federal Bureau of Investigation, or any other law enforcement agency. If you do so, or should Mr. Padillo fail to carry out his assignment, we regretfully, but of necessity, will dispose of Mrs. McCorkle.

Mr. Padillo will be able to brief you fully about his assignment. The continued well-being of Mrs. McCorkle depends upon his willingness to cooperate. He has been uncooperative until now. We regret that we must use this method of persuasion.

I read it twice and then put it back on the coffee table. "Why Fredl?" I asked.

"Because I wouldn't do it for money and they couldn't find any other pressure. They've already tried."

"Will they kill her?"

He looked at me and his dark Spanish eyes were steady and cold and curiously without reflection. "They'll kill her no matter what I do."

"Is she dead already? Have they already killed her?"

Padillo shook his head. "No. They haven't killed her yet. They'll use her for persuasion."

I got up and walked over to the bookcase and ran a finger absently over the spines of a row of books. "Maybe I should yell," I said. "Maybe I should scream and yell and pound the wall."

"Maybe you should," he said.

"I've read that it's smarter to call the cops. Just call the cops and the FBI and let them take over. They go to school to learn about stuff like this."

"If you call them, they'll kill her. They'll be watching you. They may have your phone bugged. You'll have to meet the FBI or the police someplace. When you do, she'll die. And then all you'll have is a letter written on dimestore stationery with a rented typewriter and a dead wife."

I took down a book and looked at it. I put it back and two seconds later I couldn't remember its title. "You'd better tell me what it's all about," I said. "Then I'll decide whether to call the cops or not."

Padillo nodded and got up and went over to the bar and poured himself another drink. "I'll do anything to get her back," he said. "Anything. I'll do what they want me to do or I'll go to the police and the FBI with you—if you decide on that. Or we can try something else. You want another drink?" I nodded.

"But you have to make the decision," he continued. "You have to decide what has to be done."

He carried the drinks over to the coffee table and lowered himself carefully into a chair. He winced as he did it. The knife wound seemed to bother him.

"That night on the Rhine when I went over the side with Jimmy Ku," he said. "Jimmy had never learned to swim. He drowned. I was shot in the left arm, but I made it to shore. I was sick, I was shot and I was damned tired. I heard you when they helped you up the bank. I wasn't too far away. You finally flagged a truck, right?"

I nodded.

"It was while I was lying there that I decided to be dead for a while. I decided to be dead in Switzerland. I went to Zurich. It's easy to be dead there. You don't have to hear how I got to Switzerland."

"Let's just assume that you didn't swim."

"No. I went to Remagen first and found a doctor and then I went to Zurich. I kept in touch indirectly. I heard about the saloon getting blown up and I figured that you'd collect the insurance—we were over-insured anyway. So I sat in Zurich for a couple of months and did nothing. I was staying with a friend and the friend offered me a proposition."

"In Africa."

"That's right. Africa. West Africa. We were in his office and he had a large map. He also had a large office. It seemed to my friend that several countries in West Africa would soon be in the market for small arms and he just happened to have a couple of warehouses that were full of them and only slightly used. He ticked the countries

22

off for me: Ghana, Nigeria, Togo, Dahomey, perhaps the Cameroons, and so forth. He needed a traveling salesman. He had the list of hot prospects and all he needed really was an order-taker. If the prospects bought, fine. If they didn't, somebody else would. I would get a straight salary—a high one."

"You went," I said.

Padillo nodded. "I flew to Guinea and sort of worked my way down the coast. I took orders from one faction one day and another faction the next. The product was good and my Zurich friend knew who was ripe for what. I pushed the 7.62 millimeter stuff. He was very strong on standardizing weaponry all over Africa. I made quite a few sales. If you've been reading the papers, you know where I made them."

"I've kept up."

"The last country I was in was quiet. It was just before Independence and my friend in Zurich thought I should stick around a few months, so he arranged for me to run a saloon that belonged to one of his business associates. The saloon was about fifty miles from nowhere. It was a dull wait, but my Zurich friend was convinced that it would pay off."

"Did it?" I said.

Padillo nodded. "He had thought it would be even better than Nigeria and he was right. The military pulled a coup and those who escaped being shot made off with most of the treasury. They placed a rather large order. Togo was last on my list. It had been quiet there since Olympio was assassinated in 'sixty-three and my friend in Zurich thought things might be ripening."

He paused and took a swallow of his drink. "On my way to Togo I went through Dahomey. I sent you a card."

23

"You seemed to have had writer's cramp that day."

He smiled slightly. "Something like that. I was in this hotel in Togo—in Lomé when they dropped by to see me."

"Are they the ones who wrote the note?"

"Probably. They were trying to appear German for some reason. They made their proposition in German and I turned them down in English and they forgot about their German. Then they raised the ante—from fifty thousand dollars to seventy-five thousand. I still said no."

He paused for a moment. "There were two of them," he continued. "And they told me about myself. They told me quite a bit—even some stuff that I'd almost forgotten. They had everything about you and the saloon and me and my former employers. They even knew about the two who had defected and how we'd got them back."

"Where'd they get it?"

"Wolgemuth probably lost somebody in Berlin and whoever it was took a file with him. Wolgemuth knew a lot about us."

"Then what?"

"They talked about blackmail to me there in Lomé and I laughed at them. I said I'd just go back to Switzerland and die again. You have to have something to lose to be blackmailed and there wasn't anything they could take away from me. So they got down to that one last threat that they all use because it's supposed to make you cry. Either I agreed to do what they wanted, or I'd be dead within forty-eight hours."

"Who were you supposed to kill?"

"Their Prime Minister. They had the time and the place all picked out: Pennsylvania Avenue, a block and a half west of the White House. What's today?"

"Thursday."

"It's supposed to happen a week from tomorrow."

I found myself unable to be surprised or even concerned. I had known Padillo for a long time and together we had seen a few die. A Prime Minister would be just one more and his death would be nothing compared with what I stood to lose. That's how it seemed then because Fredl was gone and because I was afraid that she would be gone forever and I would be alone again. I was afraid that if she were dead, all the years that had gone before would add up to nothing. Yet there was no panic or frenzy or scurrying about. I just sat there with Padillo and listened to him talk about the man somebody wanted him to kill so that they wouldn't kill my wife. I wondered how Fredl was and if she had cigarettes and where she would sleep and if she were cold and what she had had for dinner.

"A week from tomorrow," I said.

"A Friday."

"And what did you tell them?"

"I told them I'd let them know and then I got out of Togo. I flew out with a fifty-year-old ex-Luftwaffe pilot who thought he was still diving Stukas. He charged me a thousand dollars to go to Liberia—Monrovia. I took the next ship out—the bucket that landed me in Baltimore."

"And they knew all about it," I said. "They knew you'd gone to Monrovia and to Baltimore and they knew about Fredl and about me."

"They knew," Padillo said. "I should have gone back to Switzerland. I carry a lot of trouble around with me."

"Who is it you're supposed to kill?"

"His name is Van Zandt. He's Prime Minister of one of the smaller south African nations—the one that followed Rhodesia in declaring its unilateral independence from Britain. The British got excited and started talking about treason and then put through some economic sanctions."

"I remember," I said. "It's before the UN now. The country has about two million people and one hundred thousand of them are whites. What else has it got?"

"A hell of a lot of chromium—about a third of our supply."

"We can't let that go."

"Not according to Detroit."

"Who wants you to kill Van Zandt? He's an old man."

"The two who approached me were from his cabinet. He's arriving here in a couple of days to make a plea before the UN. First he'll put in an appearance in Washington. There won't be any royal treatment here—just an Assistant Secretary of State to meet him at the airport and a ride down Constitution Avenue. He won't get near the White House."

"What're you supposed to do?"

"Pick him off with a rifle. They're to set it up for me."

"Won't the old man get suspicious?"

"Hardly. It's all his idea. He'll be dead of cancer within two months anyhow."

They liked to mention that Hennings Van Zandt was eighty-two years old and that he had been one of the first whites to be born in the country that he served as Prime Minister. He had watched it evolve from a virtually unexplored territory into a private preserve of the British South Africa Company, then into a colony, and finally into a self-governing country. Now he claimed it was independent, but Britain said it wasn't and that its declaration of independence was tantamount to treason. Because of the chromium, the U.S. had made only gruff warnings about not recognizing the declaration.

"When they made me the proposition, they spelled it all out," Padillo said. "I don't know if it's logical or not. All I know is that it could cause a hell of an uproar."

According to Padillo the plan was to announce that Van Zandt was coming to the U.S. to plead his country's cause before the United Nations. He would stop first in Washington for trade talks and for a try at countering the British anti-independence campaign.

"They've followed the civil rights action here," Padillo said. "Van Zandt himself came up with the idea. He gets assassinated, the blame is placed upon an unnamed American Negro, and public opinion here does a flip-flop in support of Van Zandt and his government."

"That's tricky thinking," I said, "but they sound like a tricky bunch."

"They have it all mapped out. There'll be almost no police or security protection for Van Zandt—nothing like what's laid on for De Gaulle or Wilson. They'll make sure that the Prime Minister is riding in an open car. When he's shot, he becomes a martyr in America to the cause of white supremacy, which is about as good a way to go as any if you're eighty-two, think like he does, and have a stomach that's three-fourths eaten away by cancer."

"Why did they pick you?" I said.

"They wanted a pro—someone who wouldn't get caught—because they're going to have unimpeachable eyewitnesses who saw a Negro with a rifle. They need someone who can make it down the elevator, out into the lobby, and across the street. They picked me."

"Could you do it?"

Padillo held up his glass to the light and looked at it as

if it contained an unfriendly cockroach. "I suppose so. I could do it and feel nothing. Zero. I think that's what I'm most afraid of. It's been getting a little empty. But say the word and I'll do it and I won't get caught and you might get your wife back."

"Might?"

"She'll be dead, of course, but they could let you live long enough to bury her."

"You don't think they'd like to have me walking around with all my inside knowledge?"

"Neither you nor Fredl nor me. The two who made me the proposition are to be the eyewitnesses. If you include Van Zandt, that's a conspiracy of three and that's damned big for something like this."

"With us, it's six," I said.

"That's why they won't want us around."

I looked at my watch. It was almost three in the morning and the apartment seemed to be assuming the impersonal quality of one of the rooming houses that had once stood in its place. Padillo was sitting in the chair, his drink on the coffee table, his head in his hands. He seemed to be giving the rug a careful examination.

"I should have gone to Switzerland," he said again.

"But you didn't."

"I wasn't very smart. I must be getting old. I feel old."

"You're two months younger than I am."

"So what do you want me to do? Go down to the FBI with you or take out my Husqvarna with the 7x scope and pop away at the old man?"

"If I go to the police, they'll kill her," I said.

"Yes."

"I don't want her killed. I don't want me killed. I don't even want you killed which proves how generous I'm getting now that the shock's wearing off. But they'll kill all three of us if you shoot him."

"I can almost guarantee that they'll kill you and Fredl," Padillo said. "It might take longer for me, but then they're not so much concerned about me because I'm not the kind to turn myself in for the murder of a visiting Prime Minister. They could take their time, but they'd put someone on it and someday I'd get careless or he'd get lucky."

"They knew I'd figure it out," I said. "They knew I'd realize that they wouldn't want Fredl or me around after the assassination. They may know I'm not overly bright, but they must also know that I'm not that thick."

Padillo took his head out of his hands and looked at me. "It's your turn to get the drinks," he said. "My side hurts."

I got up and went over to the bar and mixed two more.

"They don't think you're thick," he said. "They just think you suffer from something called hope—hope that they won't kill Fredl if I kill Van Zandt, hope that they won't kill you, and hope that you'll be able to outsmart them. Hope even that they'll change their minds and call it all off because it's raining that day." He paused for a moment. "But they believe that the only hope you really believe in is for me to kill him."

"And you'd do it?"

"You call it."

"There's nothing else I can do." I made it a statement, but I meant it as a question.

Padillo examined his glass for trespassers again. "Maybe I'm getting the DTs," he said, "or maybe it was my African vacation. I've got the habit of looking for strangers." He took a swallow of the drink. "There's one thing that can be done," he said.

"What?"

"Try to get her back before they kill her."

"It's a big town," I said, "and there's half of Virginia and Maryland to consider. Where do I start, a block away or fifty miles away? Should I just call up their embassy or trade mission or whatever it is and ask if I could speak to my wife for a moment before they do her in?"

"The trouble with the Van Zandt crowd," Padillo said, "is that they don't care much for majority rule, especially if the majority happens to be black and its members live in places that make Mississippi look like Happy Valley. The Van Zandt people are a little cracked maybe, a little over-imaginative, but they're not dumb. They'd probably keep Fredl where you wouldn't think of looking for her."

"In the briar patch, Br'er Fox?"

"Exactly, Br'er Rabbit."

"In a Negro district."

"It's a possibility."

"There're only about a couple hundred thousand places where she could be."

"We can look or we can sit around and drink some more Scotch."

"What do you suggest?"

"This Hardman," Padillo said. "How well do you know him?"

"Well enough. He's a regular customer of mine and I'm a regular customer of his."

"I didn't know you were using."

"Just some slow horses."

"He know Fredl?"

"Fairly well. He likes her. She once did a story on him."

"You're seeing him tomorrow?"

"At one-fifteen."

"That's one appointment. We'll make another for ten in the morning."

"With whom?"

"With somebody who can put me in touch with three debtors."

I stared at him. "What do they owe you?"

Padillo grinned. "Their lives. I'm calling the loans tomorrow."

— FOUR —

I was awake by seven that morning. I was in our big double bed which featured the high intensity lamps whose bulbs seemed to burn out every other day or so. I awoke with the feeling that I had something important to do and I thought of asking Fredl what it was until I remembered that she was gone. The bed seemed far too grand for one person. When we placed the special order for it, we had three purposes in mind: making love, sleeping and reading. It had served admirably, except for the reading, and that was because of the lamps that kept going out at odd times. They used the same kind of bulbs that are used in the taillights of cars and I wondered if I shouldn't lay in a supply from the corner gas station. It might be cheaper.

It was something to debate and it took a while to decide that I should buy only one bulb as a trial. I cast around for some other trivial problem to resolve and Vietnam came to mind. But I soon gave up on that and lay in the big bed and stared up at the off-white ceiling and thought about Fredl. You can grieve when someone dies. But when someone is near death, and there is the chance that you might prevent it if you make the right decision, anxiety takes over. I fumbled on the table by the bed for a pre-breakfast cigarette which I didn't want and wouldn't enjoy but perversely lighted. I continued to lie in the bed and smoke the cigarette and make important decisions. I decided to go to the FBI. A few moments later I decided to let Padillo shoot the Prime Minister. When I began to plan my arrival at the White House where I would dramatically dump my problem into the lap of a concerned but admiring President, I got up and went into the bathroom.

I looked at the face in the mirror and blew some smoke at it, but the smoke came out the wrong way and I started coughing. It was either lung cancer or emphysema. Probably both. The coughing finally went away and I could look in the mirror again. The face that was there said, "You stink, McCorkle." I nodded wearily and turned on the shower.

When I was dressed in my bankers' grey flannel with the carefully muted chalk stripes that were supposed to take ten pounds off my weight, I headed for the kitchen. On the way, I knocked on the door of the guest bedroom where I could hear Padillo stirring. At least he didn't whistle. In the kitchen I heated water for the instant coffee. I was drinking my first cup when Padillo came in wearing his Good Will clothes. I indicated the boiling teakettle and the coffee and he nodded and mixed a cup. He sat down at the table and sipped it.

"You have a couple of suitcases worth of clothes hanging in a closet down at the Mayflower," I said.

"Fredl?"

"She had everything in your apartment in Bonn packed and shipped over. Most of it's in storage, but she kept out some stuff. She says you have better taste than I do."

"She has the reporter's eye."

"You're also half-owner in a saloon not too far from here which you might like to drop in on someday."

Padillo stirred his coffee carefully and then lighted a cigarette. It was probably his first that morning. "I have no claim, Mac."

"Some people might not think so, but you spent about ten years of your life running the one we had in Bonn when you weren't out chasing Helmut Dantine or whoever. And where else would you get a job at your age?"

"That's a thought. What's the setup?"

"It seats about one-twenty not counting the bar. I brought Karl over as head bartender and Herr Horst is *maitre d'* and I upped his cut to six percent of the net. He's worth it. We've got twelve waiters, two cocktail girls, busboys and the kitchen help run by a better-than-fair chef whom I found in New York. He's better than fair when he's sober anyhow, which is most of the time. The waiters are on a split shift. We open at eleven-thirty and close at two a.m., except midnight on Saturday because then it's the Sabbath which we don't stay open for."

"Are we making money?"

"It's not bad. We can go over the books later."

"Who's the crowd?"

"I jacked up the prices and they seem willing to pay for the service and the food. Not much tourist stuff except from the conventions. Some press, some Capitol Hill types, some military, some business and public relations operators, association executives, bored housewives, and a lot of repeat trade from customers we had in Bonn. That embassy crowd moves around together and they like to show off their German."

"Can it run itself?"

"As long as Horst is around."

Padillo nodded. "What's the suite at the Mayflower for?"

"For you. It's in your name. It was Fredl's idea, although basically I'm thoughtful and kind, too. She didn't take to the idea of the Rhine eels nibbling at you so when we got the postcard, she suggested the suite. It's been a good idea because we've been able to help people out when the town's jammed. It's also a logical business expense. Even Internal Revenue agrees. And you have to have a Washington address."

I suppose we talked about business because we didn't want to talk about Fredl or what might happen to her, but the words I said to Padillo were said by rote, as if I were an economics professor lecturing to a dull freshman class on a warm spring day.

We had another cup of coffee and Padillo asked: "You usually get up this early?"

"I didn't sleep much."

"Worried?"

"Near panic, but not there yet. Just near."

He nodded. "I don't blame you. It's just as well we got up early; there's a lot to be done."

"Where do we start?"

"I'd say at the Mayflower. We have to go calling this morning and the lady we're calling on used to be particular about the way people dressed."

"How's your side?"

"It's sore," he said. "But it isn't deep. I'll get some stuff and change the bandages this afternoon."

I put the dishes in the sink and turned off the stove and we rode the elevator to the lobby.

"It goes to the basement," Padillo said. "What's down there?"

"The garage."

"Attendant on duty?"

"No. You park your own."

"They probably went in and came out that way. With Fredl."

"Probably."

"What are you driving, something flashy?"

"A Stingray. Fredl remained loyal. She has a Volks."

"Do you really need a car?"

"Not really, but I suffer from self-indulgence."

"How do you get to work?"

"Walk."

"How far is the Mayflower from here?"

"Walking distance, but considering your enfeebled condition, we'll take a cab."

We found a cab and crept the six blocks to the Mayflower, our driver snarling at the lousy driving of the stream of stern-faced government employees. The government employees snarled back. Eight-fifteen in the morning in Washington is not a happy time.

"Bastards gonna make me late for work," our driver said as he pulled up in front of the hotel.

"Where do you work?" I asked.

"Department of Agriculture." He didn't seem to expect a tip but I gave him a quarter anyway and he bulldozed his way out into traffic and started snarling at his fellow employees again.

I introduced Padillo to an assistant manager of the hotel. I didn't make any excuses for the clothes or the three-day beard. If they didn't like a bum for a guest, we would find another hotel. But the assistant manager didn't blink and gave Padillo a warm welcome. I asked that breakfast for two be sent up and we caught the elevator.

It was a two-room suite, neither plain nor fancy. It looked as if it had had its share of parties and most of the exposed wooden surfaces were covered with glass or had been finished in drink- and cigarette-resistant plastic. Padillo walked over to the closet and opened it. There were several suits, a couple of jackets, some slacks, a sweater and a light top coat.

"She picked out the ones I like best," he said.

"There are shirts and socks and stuff in a drawer. I think I remember a shaving kit, too."

He found what he needed and disappeared into the bathroom. When he came out he was wearing a white oxford-cloth with a black knit tie, a single breasted suit of a soft grey herringbone weave, and black pebble-grained plain-toed oxfords.

"With that tan you look as if you're just back from Miami."

"I was thinking of a mustache, but it would make me look too dashing."

"You'll do fine with our young matron crowd."

Padillo looked around the room. There wasn't much to see: a couch, a coffee table, three easy chairs, a television set, the usual writing desk with a glass top, two or three straight chairs, some lamps, a rug with a spastic floral pattern, and some pictures on the wall that pretended to represent the seasons in some bucolic land that the artist only half remembered. I also counted eight ashtrays.

"Home," Padillo said.

"How long has it been now?"

"More than ten years."

"And you get knifed the minute you step off the boat."

"It wasn't till then that I was sure I was really back home." .

There was a knock at the door and I told Padillo it was the breakfast. He opened the door, but it wasn't breakfast; it was a pair of young men who looked friendly and confident and as if they'd like to be helpful. One of them smiled and asked for Mr. Padillo.

"I'm Mr. Padillo."

"I'm Charles Weinriter and this is Lee Iker," one of them said. He was the taller by an inch. "We're with the Federal Bureau of Investigation." They both produced the folding black books that contained their identification and passed them to Padillo just like it says to do in the regulations.

Padillo looked at his watch. Fredl must have placed it in his shaving kit. He hadn't been wearing it earlier. "It took you about twenty minutes to get here from the time the hotel called," he said. "That's quite good considering the traffic."

"We'd like to talk to you a few minutes, Mr. Padillo," Weinriter said.

"I bet you would."

"Would it be possible to do it alone?"

"No," Padillo said and smiled. "No, it wouldn't be possible at all. In fact, you can consider yourself lucky to talk to me in the presence of a witness. His name is Mr. McCorkle and he's my partner."

I was sitting in an easy chair with one foot dangling over an arm. I waved at them. "My pleasure."

They nodded at me from the doorway, but they didn't seem to be as friendly as before.

"Do you have any means of identification, Mr. Padillo?" Iker asked.

"No, I don't," Padillo said. "But come on in. Maybe we can work something out with a game of twenty questions."

They came in. Padillo indicated the couch and they sat on it gingerly. Padillo eased himself into one of the arm chairs. His side still seemed to hurt.

"We've sent down for coffee," he said and smiled another pleasant smile. "It should be here shortly."

"You don't have any identification?" Weinriter asked.

"None. Is that unusual? Of course, my partner here can identify me. If you can believe he's who he says he is."

"I have identity," I said. "I know who I am."

"I have an idea," Padillo said. "I'll be right back." He went into the bathroom and came back holding an empty water glass. "Here," he said to Iker and tossed him the glass. Iker's reflexes were fast; he caught it.

"Don't smudge the prints," Padillo said. "If you run the prints on that glass through your computer downtown, you'll find a full file on me. Incidentally, there's a careful thumb-print on the bottom of the glass. It shouldn't take long and that file on me goes back to when I was sixteen years old."

Iker set the glass down carefully on the coffee table. "You don't seem to care much for the FBI, Mr. Padillo."

"Is that one of the questions you have to ask me?"

"No," Iker said. "It's just a comment."

"You've been out of the country a long time," Weinriter said.

"More than ten years."

"You arrived here yesterday?"

"Yes."

39

"Where did you enter the country, Mr. Padillo?"

"Baltimore."

"You arrived by plane or ship?"

"Ship."

"Which one?"

There was another knock at the door. This time I got it and it was the room-service man with breakfast. He wheeled the tray in briskly and had a cheery good morning for us all. "Told me there were only going to be two of you. Just two. But I brought cups for four. I always do. It'll be just a moment now." He snapped the leaves of the wheeled table into place, reached underneath and brought out the portable warming oven.

"Everybody wants coffee right now, I bet." He was a short, bustling man with a rogue's eyes and a leprechaun's mouth. The mouth seemed to have an endless supply of chatter. He put four cups on the table and filled them. He put spoons in the saucers. "Coffee coming up, gentlemen. Nothing like a good cup to begin the day. Here you are, sir," he said to Iker. Iker accepted the cup and looked as if he had compromised the Bureau. Weinriter got the next cup and the third and fourth went to Padillo and me. The waiter served sugar and cream. Padillo took cream; I accepted sugar. Iker and Weinriter were of sterner stuff and drank theirs black.

The room-service waiter bustled around some more, spooning the scrambled eggs and bacon onto plates, making sure the butter was cold, hard and unspreadable in its bed of ice, and that the toast was cool enough to eat. Then he presented the check with a flourish to Weinriter who looked embarrassed for a moment until I said, "The gentleman over there will sign for it." The waiter almost trotted over to Padillo who signed the check.

"You need anything else, you just call me, number forty-two," said the waiter.

"You have a name?" Padillo asked.

"I'm Al, sir."

"If we need anything, we'll call you, Al."

"Thank you, sir."

I rose and walked to the table on wheels. "You don't mind if we go ahead?" I said to Iker and Weinriter. They shook their heads to indicate that they didn't mind. Padillo sat across the table from me. He put some cold butter on his cool toast. I tried the eggs. They were quite good.

"Which ship, Mr. Padillo?"

"The *Frances Jane*."

"Were you a passenger?"

"Yes."

"You weren't on the passenger list."

"I was traveling incognito. Look under Billy Joe Thompson."

"May I see your passport?" Iker said.

Padillo picked up a piece of bacon, took a bite, and chewed it slowly. Then he took a sip of coffee. "I don't have one."

"How did you get on the ship without a passport?"

"They didn't ask me for one. The *Frances Jane* is no cruise liner, friend. It's a tramp."

"What happened to your passport, Mr. Padillo?"

"I lost it."

"Have you reported the loss to the State Department?"

"No. I didn't think they would be interested."

Weinriter tried some sarcasm. I felt sorry for him. "I think the State Department might be just a little interested in the loss of your passport, Mr. Padillo."

After he borrowed a cigarette from me Padillo leaned

back in the chair and looked at Iker and Weinriter. He took his time. "If you want to report the loss of a passport with the name Michael Padillo on it to the State Department, go ahead. They'll have no record of it ever being issued. If I needed a passport, there's an outfit in Detroit that would provide one in twenty-four hours along with a brand new driver's license, a registration card, and a social security number that would check out just fine on the big computer in Baltimore. But you probably know all this and if you do, then you also know that my attorneys in Bonn have filed income tax returns for me for the last ten years and if you have any questions about those, you'll have to get in touch with them. Now is there anything else?"

"Whom do you work for, Mr. Padillo?" Weinriter said.

"For myself. I help run a bar and restaurant."

"That's not what I mean."

"Then try it again."

"Who sent you to Africa?"

"I was on vacation. It took my life's savings, but it was worth it."

"We have different information."

"Hang on to it."

"It says you were selling arms."

"It's wrong."

"It's a serious charge, Mr. Padillo. You seem to think it's a joke."

"It's not very serious or you wouldn't be sitting here just mumbling about it. You'd have a Federal warrant and I'd be on my way downtown. You don't have a warrant and I suspect you're working somebody else's territory and if they find out about it, they'll get all nervous and worked up and indignant again."

"You mean?" I said as they used to say it on radio about three o'clock in the afternoon.

"The very same, Inspector," Padillo said. "The notorious CIA."

"That puts an entirely different light on the matter, doesn't it, Reggie?" I said.

"You two are very funny," Iker said. "You're also a waste of time. We know about you, Padillo, and we know about your partner here. You're right. There is a file on both of you. A thick one." He stood up. Weinriter joined him. "I have the feeling that it's going to get a lot thicker."

They moved towards the door. Just as they had it open, Padillo said, "You forgot the evidence." He tossed the water glass with the fingerprints. Iker used his reflexes again and fielded it nicely. He looked at it, looked at Padillo, and shook his head. He put the glass down on the table. "You two are very funny," he said again.

When they left they closed the door quietly behind them.

— FIVE —

"What brought that on?" I asked.

"The hotel probably had instructions to call as soon as I made an appearance," Padillo said. "They just dropped by to make sure it was me. They'll be back from time to time."

"That casual visit could get Fredl killed."

"I doubt it. They're trained not to be spotted, but we can do without the social calls. We'll move fast now."

He walked over to the telephone and dialed a number. When it answered he spoke rapidly in Spanish. He was going far too quickly for me, but I could tell that he was speaking a classy Castillian. The conversation lasted about three minutes. Padillo hung up the phone and turned to me.

"We have an appointment in half an hour."

"Is this the woman who likes her visitors all spruced up?"

He nodded. "She's growing old, but she likes nice things. Money's about the nicest thing she knows."

"This one's going to cost, I take it?"

Padillo shook his head. "I don't think so. I think she'll do it for sentiment. She was in love with my old man once, a long time ago."

"In Spain?"

He nodded. "When he got killed in Madrid, she made arrangements to get my mother and me to Portugal and then to Mexico City." Padillo's mother had been a beauty from Estonia who had married a Spanish attorney. The attorney had been shot by the winners in 1937. Mother and son had gone to Mexico where she had supported them by giving piano and language lessons. She taught Padillo to speak six or seven languages perfectly before she died of tuberculosis in the early 1940's. I don't think he could play the piano. He had told me all this a long time ago in Bonn when we first met. It was this unique fluency with languages that had drawn him to the attention of the U.S. spy crowd.

"What's your father's old flame do now?"

"She keeps track of others who are still in my former line of work."

"You know her well?"

"Very. I've seen her quite a few times over the years."

"She won't peddle what you know?"

"We won't tell her what I know."

We took a cab to a quiet neighborhood in Chevy Chase, just inside the District line, where Senora Madelena de Romanones did whatever she did for a living. It was a two-story house, built in the style of the 'thirties with a shingled roof and red brick that was painted white. The white paint was flaking a little, but they may have planned it that way. A screened porch was on the left and some large elms in the well-kept yard gave enough shade so that the porch looked as if it would be pleasantly cool in summer. I paid the cab and we walked up to the front door and rang the chimes. We could hear them sounding inside and a dog began to bark. It sounded like a small dog. A Negro maid opened the door.

"We wish to see Senora de Romañones," Padillo said. "I'm Mr. Padillo; this is Mr. McCorkle."

"Miz Romanones is spectin you," the maid said. She unlatched the screen door and held it open for us. We went in and followed her down an entrance hall. She stopped at a pair of sliding doors and opened them. Padillo went through first.

The woman wasn't as old as I had expected. She must have been around thirty when she was in love with Padillo's father for she was no more than sixty now and in the dim light of the drawing room she could pass for fifty. She was erect in a wine-colored chair and smiled at Padillo as he crossed the room and bent over her hand. "May I present my colleague, Mr. McCorkle," he said.

I bowed over her hand, too, and she said that she was enchanted. There was a network of ridged blue veins on the back of her hand that gave it a slightly arthritic look. The rings on her fingers I estimated at close to ten thousand dollars.

"You will join me in coffee, Michael; you and Mr. McCorkle?"

"Thank you."

"You can serve the coffee now, Lucille," she said to the maid who stood in the doorway.

The maid said "Yes, ma'am," and left. Padillo and I

took two chairs that faced Senora de Romanones across an inlaid table whose curved legs ended in lions' heads that held round glass balls in their mouths. The rest of the furniture was of the same period, whatever it was. Dark wood glistened with polish and use. The floor was covered with oriental rugs that overlapped and the dusty-rose walls were hung with somber oil portraits of family or friends or just strangers whose features were obscured by the dimness of the room. A Knabe piano was tucked into one corner. Its keys were exposed, its lid was open, there was sheet music on its stand, and it looked as if somebody might have been playing it just before we arrived. The outside world was kept out by drawn maroon velvet curtains. Sunlight probably did nothing for either the oriental rugs or for the fine network of lines in the face and neck of Senora de Romanones.

"It has been such a long time, Michael," she said. "I despaired of seeing you again." She had a curiously penetrating voice, not loud, but well-toned and full of command.

"It was three years ago in Valencia," Padillo said.

"Do you speak Spanish, Mr. McCorkle?"

"Not well, I'm afraid."

"His German is excellent," Padillo said. "If you would prefer——"

She smiled slightly. "I remain cautious, Michael. So we shall speak German.

"Usually, Michael, you come to see me only when you have some dreary task at hand."

"I am grateful for the tasks, because they give me the opportunity to be with you."

She laughed. "Give me a cigarette. The way you turn

47

a compliment reminds me of your father. He was such an articulate man, although his politics was pathetic."

"Yet you helped him many times, Madelena. And my mother."

She waved the cigarette that Padillo had given her. "I helped him because I foolishly was in love with him despite the fact that he was married. I helped your mother because of you. I never liked her really. She was too beautiful, too intelligent, too good." She paused for a moment and smiled. "Too much competition, I suppose."

The maid came in with a tray containing a silver coffee service and some almost translucent cups. Senora de Romanones poured and the maid passed us the cups.

"That will be all, Lucille."

"Yes, ma'am," she said and left, closing the double doors behind her.

"So how do you like it, Michael, my little not-quite-suburban nest?"

"I was surprised when I heard that you had left Madrid. I was even more surprised when I learned that you had come to Washington. I can see you in New York, Madelena, but not Washington."

She waved her cigarette around again. She did it gracefully. "This, my dear young man, is where things take place nowadays. Once it was Berlin and once it was Madrid and once it was London. Now it is either Washington or Hong Kong. I think I much prefer Washington."

"Business is good, I take it?"

"Excellent," she said. "I've rediscovered many old friends here and I have made a number of new ones. There are some mutual acquaintances whom we could have great fun gossiping about sometime."

"Nothing would be more enjoyable, but there is a deadline and once again I need your help."

She sighed and put her cigarette out carefully. "This time I will charge you, Michael. In the past I have helped you for foolish sentimental reasons, but this time you will pay. The price: Spend one hour soon with an old friend and listen to her memories."

"You would be paying me," Padillo said. "It will be a rare privilege and we will do it quite soon."

She looked at him and smiled slightly. "You even lie like your father. You are not yet married?"

"No."

"Then I will be the matchmaker. You are a wonderful catch, and I will find you a rich bride."

"I will be in debt to your ability as well as to your good taste."

"Now, what is it that you wish to know?"

"I want to locate—today, if possible—three persons."

"Are they in the States?"

"So I've heard."

"Their names?"

"Philip Price, Jon Dymec, Magda Shadid."

"A mixed bag, Michael," she said in English. "An Englishman, a Pole, and Magda, half-Syrian, half-Hungarian. I didn't realize you knew her."

"We've met. Are they in town?"

"Two of them are, Magda and Price. Dymec is temporarily in New York."

"Can you get word to them?"

"I can."

"Today."

"Yes."

"Just tell them I'm at the Mayflower, and that I'm calling my loan."

"Do you know these persons, Herr McCorkle?"

"No. They're Mike's friends."

"Take my advice. Keep it that way." She turned to Padillo. "You know, Michael, that you have piqued my curiosity and you know that I will eventually learn everything."

Padillo turned on the smile he used to charm old ladies and snakes. "In such affairs, Madelena, the fewer who know, the less the chance for future recriminations and shattered friendships. I promise you—at the earliest opportunity—"

"Ach! Michael, you have made your promises before, but the facts I've had to read in *Die Welt* or *The Times* or *Le Monde*. By the time you return, the news will be old. You know I like the details—the grisly parts that never get printed."

"This time I swear to you—"

"I will do as you say. I will be in touch with Price, Dymec and Shadid. Since you know who they are, you know what they are, and I do not have to warn you. It is an exceedingly strange combination. Do they know each other?"

"I have no idea," Padillo said.

"You are the common denominator then?"

"Yes."

"And I should not mention one to another?"

"No."

"Consider it done." She rose. "I shall see you to the door." She paused by Padillo and put her hand on his arm and turned to me. "Mr. McCorkle, the persons that Michael wishes me to reach are most dangerous and, I should add, most untrustworthy."

Padillo grinned. "What she's trying to say is that they're crooks who would peddle their aunts. Mac doesn't know anyone like that, Madelena. He lives among those of noble thoughts and kindly deed."

"His face makes you out a liar, Michael," she said looking at me with clear dark eyes. "You have to travel a far distance to acquire a face like that."

I bowed over her hand again and Padillo said: "I am in your debt."

"And I in yours, my young friend. Do not forget your promise this time."

"I could not," Padillo said.

The maid opened the door for us and I asked her to call a taxi.

"Goodbye, Mr. McCorkle," Senora Romanones said. "I like your suit." I turned to say goodbye and the light caught her just right. She was wearing a simple blue dress and her face was shadowed so that lines had disappeared. It was a remarkably well-boned face with full lips and eyes that seemed almost Eurasian. She had been stunning at one time. Then the light started to change, and she began to pull the doors together. They closed before the illusion of young beauty vanished.

We waited outside for the cab. "She's getting old," Padillo said. "It's funny, but she's one person who never seemed to age during all the years I've known her."

"Does she know all the people she says she knows?"

"She knows everybody."

"Maybe that's why she's getting old."

— SIX —

I told the cab driver that we wanted to go to Mac's Place and for once I wasn't asked the address. That brightened the morning. We took Connecticut Avenue all the way and Padillo had a fine time trying to spot a familiar landmark. He didn't find too many. "There used to be a church there," he said at the corner of Connecticut and N. "It was ugly as sin, but it had a lot of style."

"First Presbyterian. There was some talk about having it classified as a national monument or something, but nothing came of it. The offer was too high for the elders to ignore."

"Predestination, I suppose."

"Something like that. Maybe God intended it to be a parking lot."

I told the driver to let us off across the street from the saloon. "You can drink it all in," I told Padillo. We got out and he gave it a long appraising stare. "Nice," he said. "Real nice."

It was a two-story building of vaguely Federal lines that had been built a century before. It was constructed of brick that I'd had sandblasted to its original texture. Black shutters flanked the windows which were criss-crossed with moulding that held small diamond-shaped panes of glass. A grey and black canopy ran from the door across the sidewalk to the street. The name, "Mac's Place," was white on black at the end of the canopy in appropriately discreet letters.

We crossed the street and went through the two-inch-thick slab door. "We're still saving on electricity," Padillo said when we were inside.

It was dim all right, but not so dim that the thirsty couldn't find their way to the bar that ran down the length of the lefthand side of the room. It was a good bar to sit at or to lean on. There were the usual tables and chairs and carpeted floor, but the tables were far enough apart so that the diners could wave their elbows around and talk above a whisper without being overheard.

"What's upstairs?" Padillo asked.

"Private dining rooms. They'll hold from six to twenty people."

"That's a good touch."

"It's paying off."

"What's the nut?"

I told him.

"What did you do last week?"

"About fifteen hundred above it, but it was an exceptional week."

"Is Horst here yet?"

We walked over to the day bartender. I introduced him to Padillo and then asked him to find Horst. The thin, ascetic man marched quickly in from the kitchen where

53

he probably had been holding fingernail inspection. He blinked and almost lost a step when he saw Padillo, but recovered quickly.

"Herr Padillo, it is very good to see you," he said in German.

"It's nice to be back, Herr Horst. Things go well for you?"

"Very well, thank you. And with you?"

"Quite well, thanks."

"Herr Padillo will resume his active partnership, Herr Horst," I said. "Would you inform the rest of the staff?"

"Of course, Herr McCorkle. Permit me to say, Herr Padillo, that it is very good to have you back."

Padillo smiled. "It's good to be with friends again, Herr Horst."

Horst beamed and I prayed that he wouldn't throw us a Nazi salute. He settled for a stiff military bow and an almost imperceptible clicking of the heels. He had been a captain in the German Wehrmacht during World War II. He was Prussian and I suppose he once had been a party member, but neither Padillo nor I had ever inquired. He was an excellent *maitre d'* with a phenomenal memory for names who provided a continental touch and kept the help properly awed.

Padillo asked me where Karl was. "Up on the Hill," I said. "He's fallen for Congress. He comes on around five and spends his days keeping a box score on legislation."

Padillo looked at his watch. "It's eleven-thirty—"

"I was just going to suggest it," I said. "Would you do the honors?"

Padillo went around the bar and said: "What'll it be, pal?"

"A martini."

54

"Extra dry, pal?"

"Extra dry is twenty cents extra," I said.

"Another good touch. What do we charge for a regular martini?"

"Ninety-five cents—ninety-eight cents with tax."

"What's it do to the tips?"

"Builds them. There aren't as many dimes and nickels around, so they usually leave two-bits. The two cents' change is a sting to conscience."

Padillo mixed and poured the martinis and slid mine across the bar. It was brimful but none was spilled. I tasted it. "You haven't lost your touch."

Padillo came around to the customer's side and we sat at the end of the bar and watched the early drinkers arrive. They were the ones with luncheon dates at twelve who arrived fifteen minutes early for a couple of quick ones.

By twelve-thirty we were taking up valuable space so I led Padillo back through the kitchen, introduced him to the chef, and then we went farther back to the small room that I called the office. It had a desk and three chairs and a filing cabinet. There was also a couch that was fairly comfortable about three o'clock in the afternoon.

I sat down behind the desk. "I'm going to call Fredl's office and tell them she won't be in for a few days. Can you think up any good excuses?"

"Flu? Bad cold?"

"You're very good." I called and talked to Fredl's bureau chief and assured him it was nothing serious and promised to give her his best wishes for a speedy recovery.

"What now?" I asked.

"The tough part. We wait."

I walked over to the file and opened a drawer. "You may as well learn where I buy the hamburger," I said. For

the next hour we went over the books, the peculiarities of
our suppliers, the menu, and the help and their individual
problems. I showed Padillo how much money we owed,
to whom, and whether they allowed two per cent off if
bills were paid before the tenth or the fifth of the month.
"I ran on that two per cent discount the first three months,"
I said. "I won't buy now unless I get it."

On the way through the kitchen I had told Herr Horst
to bring Hardman back to the office when he arrived. At
twenty minutes after one there was a knock on the door.
"Herr Hardman is here," Horst said. When he stepped
through the door Hardman seemed to cut the small room's
living space in half.

"Hi, Mac. How you doin, baby?" he asked Padillo.

"Fine."

"You lookin good. That's a nice suit," Hardman said
as he sprawled on the couch and cocked his eighty-five-
dollar black calf shoes on one of the chairs. I noticed that
the shoes didn't turn up at the toes.

"Care for a drink?" Padillo asked.

"Fine with me," Hardman said. "Scotch-and-water."

"How do we get it?" Padillo asked.

"Simple," I said and picked up the telephone and dialed
one number. "Two martinis; one Scotch-and-water—the
good Scotch," I said.

We made some idle talk until the waiter came with the
drinks. Hardman took a long swallow of his. "You lookin
rough, Mac. Mush say somethin wrong when you go home
last night. Say somethin wrong with Fredl."

"That's right."

"She didn't split on you?"

"No. Somebody took her away. She didn't want to go."

The big brown man nodded his head slowly. "Now that's bad," he said. "That's real bad. What you want me to do?"

"We don't know yet. I guess we want to know whether you want to do anything."

"What you mean guess, man? Hell, Fredl's my buddy. Here," he said to Padillo, "look what she wrote about me in this Frankfurt, *Germany*, paper."

"Show him the original," I said. "He reads German and it's more impressive."

"Uh-huh," Hardman said, taking a Xeroxed copy of the article from his inside jacket pocket. "Read this right here."

Padillo read it quickly or pretended to. "That's something," he said, handing the article back. "That's really something."

"Ain't it though."

Before Hardman arrived, Padillo and I had discussed how much we should tell him. We decided that a fourth or even a half of the story would sound phony. We told him the entire thing—from Padillo's original contact with the Van Zandt people in Lomé to the note that was waiting for me when we got home the night before. We didn't tell him about Senora de Romanones.

"Then it wouldn't do no good for you to just go ahead and shoot this mother?"

"No."

"And you can't go down to Ninth and Pennsylvania and see the FBI?"

"No."

"Why don't I go down? These African cats don't know me."

"I wouldn't bet on that," Padillo said.

"Man, I'll just make a phone call, know what I mean? If you got the Feds down there, that we all payin good money for, we might as well use them. I ain't got nothin against law workin for me."

"Okay," Padillo said. "Suppose you call the FBI—or McCorkle or I call them from a phone booth. We say something like this: Prime Minister Van Zandt is coming to town and his cabinet wants me to shoot him to create sympathy for their independence. That's just my opening line. But they're trained to take complaints. They say: 'All right, we've got that, Mr. Padillo. Can you just give us a few more details?' Yes, I say, it seems that they've kidnapped my partner's wife—Fredl McCorkle—and unless I shoot the Prime Minister, they'll dispose of Mrs. McCorkle. That's about it, fellows, except that it's going to take place next Friday between two and three p.m. at the corner of Eighteenth and Pennsylvania just across the street from the United States Information Agency."

"It won't work, Hardman," I said. "If you call the FBI, they'll tighten the security to the point that Van Zandt's crowd will know something's gone wrong. If Van Zandt isn't killed—then Fredl is—automatically."

"You mean you can tell 'em the time and the place and everything and they can't do nothin?"

"That's the trouble," I said. "They can do too much. They can save the Prime Minister, but my wife gets killed. I won't make the trade."

"So you gonna do it private?"

"We're going to try."

"Think we could get another drink and some lunch?" Hardman said.

"I've saved you a nice steak," I said and picked up the phone and ordered. The drinks came first and when the waiter was gone, Hardman said: "How you want to fit me in?"

"You know this town," I said. "And you have friends who know it even better. We have a wild idea. It's possible that Van Zandt's people are hiding Fredl in some Negro neighborhood. They might figure it's the last place anyone would look. This is only a guess, but you've got ins with maids, liquor store delivery men, service people—guys who go in and out of dozens of houses a day. Maybe you can find out if they've spotted anything unusual, or if they've seen Fredl."

"I'll have to use Mush."

"How much do you have to tell him?"

"Some. Not all. But some. He was with you when you got home last night."

"What do you think?" Padillo asked.

Hardman leaned forward on the couch, looked at the floor, and sucked thoughtfully on a hollow tooth. "I don't think much of your idea that she's hid out in a colored section. But, hell, that ain't hard to check. Hard thing's goin to be to check out the white sections. But like you say, they might have a maid. Don't this outfit have a front man in town—an embassy or something?"

"They have a trade mission," Padillo said.

"I'd sure look those mothers up. They must know something."

"We plan to."

The waiter arrived with the lunch and we ate without much further conversation. When we were on the second cup of coffee, Hardman leaned back and sighed. "Mac, you serve about the best goddamned steak in town. And you have to pay about the highest price to get it."

"Keeps out the riffraff."

The big man got up and stretched. "I best be goin. I'll

59

get in touch with you later this evenin. Where you gonna be?"

Padillo gave him the number of his suite at the Mayflower and said: "We may need a place to meet with some friends. Some place private. You have any ideas?"

"How bout Betty's where you was last night?"

"Think she'd object?"

"Baby, long's I pay the rent she ain't gonna object too much."

"Fine."

"I'll call you . . . You think they got your line at the Mayflower bugged?"

Padillo shrugged. "I'll play it cozy," Hardman said. "Might even send Mush around to give you the word." He found a toothpick in his shirt pocket, stuck it in his mouth, gave us a casual wave, and was gone.

"That's a start," I said.

"That's about all you can call it."

"Have any suggestions?"

"Go back to the hotel and wait for the phone to ring."

"The hard part."

"That's right," he said. "Waiting. The hardest part of all."

We walked to the Mayflower and caught the elevator. Padillo fitted his key in the door of his suite, turned it, and we went in. The man was sitting on the couch, his hands carefully in view.

"I'm Evelyn Underhill," he said. "I mean no harm, and I have no weapon. I wish to talk to you."

Padillo tossed his key on the coffee table. "You pick the lock?"

"It's not a difficult one. Locks are a hobby."

"Who are you, Mr. Underhill?"

"I'm a fellow countryman of Hennings Van Zandt."

I moved over to him quickly. "Do you know where my wife is?"

"You're Mr. McCorkle?"

"Yes. Who are you?"

"Evelyn Underhill. I was a member of our Parliament until Prime Minister Van Zandt dissolved it. I suppose you could call me a voice of reason. There are a few of us there—a minority within a minority, so to speak."

"You're not clear," Padillo said.

"You're Mr. Padillo, aren't you? I saw you from a distance in Lomé."

"I'm Padillo, you're Underhill, and he's McCorkle. We know why we're here. We don't know why you are."

He smiled faintly; there was just a touch of humor in it. "I'm usually more coherent, but the trip was exhausting." He was a slight man, about fifty, with small bones and long grey hair combed back. The tweed suit he wore looked old and worn and rumpled. He fumbled in one of his jacket pockets and produced a pipe and a pouch of tobacco. "Do you mind if I smoke?" he asked. He wore glasses with gold rims and his pale blue eyes turned to each of us as he asked the question. His voice sounded British.

"Go ahead." There was no use rushing him. He would tell it in his own time and his own way.

He got the pipe going with three matches. "Perhaps I should first summarize it all for you and then supply the details. There are certain fellow citizens of mine who have financed my trip here. They are members of that small minority of reason which I mentioned—at least we like to think that we are." He puffed away on his pipe some more.

"My mission here is really quite simple: I'm to prevent Mr. Padillo from assassinating the Prime Minister."

— SEVEN —

I turned to Padillo and couldn't keep the exasperation out of my voice. "It was going to be a conspiracy of three, you said, but an official, revised estimate later put it at six: just Van Zandt and a few cronies, you said. Now we're well past six with the rest of Underhill's precinct still to be heard from. Christ, this is no conspiracy; it's a convention."

"I didn't sign on to be clairvoyant," Padillo said. "Just clever."

"I'm edgy."

"I notice."

He pulled a chair over by Underhill, sat down on it, and lighted a cigarette. "You saw me in Lomé?"

The thin man nodded through a haze of pipe tobacco that mingled with the smoke from Padillo's cigarette. His blue eyes blinked rapidly behind his glasses. "At the hotel just after they talked to you."

"You know them?"

"Grew up with them."

"And you think they tried to hire me to kill your Prime Minister?"

"Know it for a fact." He puffed away on his pipe some more, and then used it to gesture with. "You see, Mr. Padillo, the white community in my country is very small—around a hundred thousand or so. People in government tend to compose an even smaller community. It might be called a minor establishment. We're not very good at this espionage business, you know. Haven't had the experience, for one thing. But the information about you was obtained from what I believe is usually described as an unimpeachable source."

"What was the source?"

This time the blue eyes fairly twinkled. "My wife," Underhill said and grinned and went on hurriedly: "You remember the chap who called on you at the hotel in Lomé and said his name was Kraus. He was the taller of the two, pretended to be German and later admitted that he was really the Minister of Transport?"

"I remember him," Padillo said.

"Well, the poor fellow simply couldn't bear to keep the adventure to himself. Went back and told his wife the whole thing after making her swear a black oath of secrecy."

"But she talked?"

"Of course."

"To whom?"

"To her sister—my wife."

Padillo got up and walked around the room. "Can we order some liquor up here?" he asked me.

"Just pick up the phone and tell room service to send up a fifth and some ice."

He picked up the phone and placed the order. Then he turned to Underhill again.

"You said you saw me in Lomé—from a distance. Why were you in Lomé?"

"I was keeping an eye on the pair that approached you. Mr. Padillo, I must again stress that ours is a small white community among some two million natives. There are a number of us who are determined that the entire country shall not be plunged into social and economic chaos because of the stubbornness and hatred and even cruelty of other whites. We have collected a sum of money—some of us donated savings, others of us mortgaged property—and we intend to use this fund to prevent that old fool Van Zandt from becoming a martyr. If you were to kill him, it would send us headlong into a blood bath. I'm a professor of Romance languages at our university, so I may not be skilled at the proper way to go about conducting such negotiations as these, but I am prepared to offer you seventeen thousand pounds not to kill Van Zandt. It may not be as much as they are offering, but it is all we could raise. If you reject our offer and accept the assassination assignment, then I must discover a way of killing you."

"Why don't you just go to the police?" I said. "Or to the FBI. Has everybody stopped taking from them?"

"That must be an Americanism," Underhill said.

"Sort of," Padillo said.

"To be perfectly honest, I haven't been to your police or FBI because we simply don't want them—or anyone in your government—to learn about the plot right now. It's weird enough as it stands, but if your government were to discover the details, they would approach the Prime Minister when he arrives. He would deny the entire thing, and that would be the end of it.

"You see, gentlemen, we want the attempt to be made, but we want it to fail. Even more important, we must obtain proof that the plot was hatched, directed and paid for by Van Zandt and supporters. We are prepared to offer you the seventeen thousand pounds to do this for us, Mr. Padillo—and Mr. McCorkle, of course."

"Your friends in Lomé made a similar proposition," Padillo said. "They said they'd kill me if I didn't assassinate the Prime Minister. They made that promise after I turned down their previous proposition involving a sum of dollars which amounted to somewhat more than you're offering."

Underhill nodded his head. "Yes, they're a bloodthirsty lot. I must confess that I have no idea about how I'd go about doing it. Killing you, I mean. What is their latest offer?"

"They've offered to kill my wife if Padillo doesn't kill Van Zandt," I said. "They've kidnapped her."

"Dear me. That does put you in an awkward position, doesn't it?"

There was a knock on the door and Al, the room-service waiter, bustled in with the bottle of Scotch, the glasses and the ice. He wanted to know how we were and we told him we were fine. Padillo signed the check and Al went out the door trailing a string of "Thank you, sirs" behind him. I poured the drinks and asked Underhill if he wanted ice in his. He said no.

"Mr. Underhill," Padillo said. "I have no intention of killing your Prime Minister."

"Delighted to hear it. Although I must say that you have a most impressive record in that sort of thing."

"What makes you think so?"

"There was this chap from Berlin who looked us up and

offered to sell us the same information that he'd sold Van Zandt's people. Charged us two hundred pounds. Lord knows how much Van Zandt and that crowd paid. The information was about you—a rather extensive dossier, I should add. Mr. McCorkle was mentioned, too. You owned a restaurant together in Bonn, I believe."

The conversation was skittering from topic to topic. Either Underhill was a first rate dissembler, or he had one of the least organized minds I'd run across. I tried to get back on a pertinent course. "Mr. Underhill, do you have any idea who has my wife and where they may be keeping her?"

"I can probably make a very good guess as to who has her. There's a chance that I can give you some information as to where she's being held. But it would seem that's a rather good bargaining point for me, wouldn't you say?"

"I suggest that you not bargain with Mr. McCorkle about his wife," Padillo said.

"No, I suppose not. It's a terribly cruel thing to do."

"But not as cruel as what Mr. McCorkle will do to you if you don't tell him."

"Who has her?" I said.

"Wendell Boggs and Lewis Darragh, most probably."

"Who are they?"

"One's Minister of Transport; the other's Minister of Home Affairs. They're the ones who met with Mr. Padillo in Lomé."

"You're saying that two of your cabinet Ministers have my wife?"

"Probably did the kidnapping, too. They're both fairly young chaps—about your age. Quite capable of anything really. I know they're both here in the country."

"Do you know where they are staying?"

"They have a secret house here in Washington, I understand. I was given the address, but it's with my gear at the hotel. Afraid I can't remember it. Have a terrible memory for figures and things like that."

"How did you learn about the house?"

"My wife told me. Boggs is my brother-in-law, you know. His wife and mine are sisters and my sister-in-law thought that Wendell was heading for grief so she confided in my wife. Wendell apparently tells his wife everything, poor fellow. I wrote the address down because I knew I would forget it and it possibly might prove useful."

"Where are you staying?"

"At the LaSalle—it's just across the street."

I made my voice slow and my tone measured. "Let's go across the street and up to your room and find the address."

"Could we then discuss my plan to botch up the attempt on Van Zandt's life?"

"We'll talk about it," Padillo said.

"I don't know what you usually get for a job of work like this, Mr. Padillo, but seventeen thousand pounds is a great deal of money in my country."

"It is in any country," Padillo said, holding the door open.

We took the zebra-striped cross walk at Connecticut and De Sales. Underhill walked slightly ahead of us at a brisk pace, puffing on his pipe, his thin arms swinging. Padillo moved more slowly, wincing slightly.

"The cut bothering you?" I asked.

Padillo started to say something but the car came out of the space in front of the drugstore and was going at least thirty-five when its bumper caught Underhill's knees and its hood found his chest and slammed him to the pavement. Padillo, slightly behind me, caught my arm and jerked me back. But it wasn't necessary. The green Ford missed me by at least two feet. It rolled over the thin grey man who taught Romance languages and who had no idea as to how he would go about killing someone. Its left rear wheel rolled over his head. The car picked up speed, slowed for a corner at L Street, turned right and disappeared. A man seated by the driver looked back once.

Padillo ignored the pain in his side and moved quickly to Underhill. A crowd formed and everyone was saying "get an ambulance," but nobody did anything about it. The pipe that Underhill had been smoking lay a foot from what had been his head. Its ashes were spilled on the pavement.

Padillo knelt by the body and his hands went quickly through the pockets. He glanced up at the circle of faces that stared down at him. He picked out one. "Call an ambulance," he said to a young man. "He's still alive." The man turned and ran towards the drugstore. Padillo rose and backed into the crowd. I was next to him. We turned and walked down the street towards K, away from the crowd.

"I got his key," Padillo said.

"Let's try it."

The LaSalle hotel is about one-third commercial offices, one-third transients, and the remaining third permanent guests who like living downtown. There are no chairs in the small lobby and no one watches who takes the automatic elevators. We took one and got off on the seventh floor and followed the numbers down to the end of the hall. Underhill had a nine-dollar room that had twin beds, an air-conditioner and a television set that was old enough not to be able to get the UHF stations. His worn pigskin suitcase was in the closet along with another tweed suit and an old Burberry raincoat. Their pockets contained nothing; neither did his suitcase.

Padillo went through the bureau drawers while I investigated the medicine cabinet in the bathroom. It had a badger hair shaving brush, soap, a toothbrush and paste, some dental floss, a set of military hairbrushes, and a comb with some grey hairs in it. The items were all neatly arranged. Underhill may have had a cluttered mind, but he kept his personal effects tidy.

Padillo found the address we were looking for in a bureau drawer. It was written in a small black Leathersmith notebook which listed Underhill's wife under the line that read: "In the event of an accident please notify:" I copied the address in Washington that we wanted and Padillo ran through the rest of the notebook quickly. "There's nothing else that seems to be of any use," he said and tossed it back in the drawer. "I did find this," he added. He held up an envelope-shaped briefcase and unsnapped it for me. It was packed with five-pound British notes done up neatly in bundles and the label on each bundle said that it contained five hundred pounds.

"The seventeen thousand," I said.

"Probably."

"Shall we take it?"

"Better us than the Van Zandt crowd," Padillo said. "We can get it back to his wife who'll know where it came from."

"She seemed to know everything."

"At least she knew about the address of the secret house. What was it?"

"The 2900 block on Cambridge Place, Northwest."

"You know where it is?"

"Vaguely. It's in Georgetown."

"That's hardly a Negro district."

"Not for the past thirty-five years or so."

"We'd better go back to my place and see if I've had any calls."

We took the elevator down and crossed Connecticut. On the other side of the street, just across from the Mayflower, a pair of D.C. Accident Investigation cars were drawn up to the curb, their red and white lights blinking and circling. Two policemen were asking questions of some persons who kept shaking their heads as if they knew nothing. Another policeman was measuring something with a tape, and another one was sprinkling sand or sawdust on what looked to be a wet spot on the pavement. Evelyn Underhill had been taken away. I found myself wondering if it had been his first trip to the United States.

We rode the elevator upstairs and as Padillo opened the door with his key we could hear the telephone ring. He crossed the room, answered it, and turned to me. "It's for you," he said.

I said hello and the voice on the other end said: "You don't seem overly concerned about the continued wellbeing of your wife, Mr. McCorkle." It was a voice that just escaped being British. It was closer to an Australian or a Cape Town accent.

"I'm concerned," I said. "Do you have my wife?"

"Yes, we do. Until now she has been quite comfortable. But you have been disobeying our instructions, Mr. McCorkle. Those instructions were quite explicit."

"Let me talk to my wife."

"You were instructed to tell no one about Mr. Padillo's assignment."

"We've told no one," I said. "I want to talk to my wife."

"You talked to Underhill."

71

"I can't help who comes into a hotel room."

"What did Underhill want, Mr. McCorkle?"

"He wanted to stay alive for one thing. Just put my wife on the phone."

"Did you tell him about Mr. Padillo's assignment?"

"We didn't have to tell him; he already knew. Somebody's wife told him; maybe it was yours. Now can I talk to mine?"

"Does Mr. Padillo plan to carry out his assignment? I must again caution you, we are deadly serious."

"Yes," I said. "He plans to carry it out, but only if I talk to my wife and find out whether she's still alive."

"Very well, Mr. McCorkle, you may say hello to Mrs. McCorkle."

"Fredl—are you all right?"

"Yes, darling, I'm all right; just terribly tired." Her voice was quiet, almost resigned.

"I'm doing everything I can. Mike's here."

"I know. I heard."

"Are they treating you all right?"

"Yes, they're treating me fine, but—" And then her voice broke off and she screamed and the man's voice came back on the phone.

"We have treated her well, up until now, Mr. McCorkle. You see, we really are in earnest."

Then he hung up.

— EIGHT —

I stood in the room and held the phone in my hand and stared at it. Then I put it back where it belonged and turned to Padillo. "They made her scream," I said. "They hurt her somehow and made her scream."

He nodded and turned away to look out the window. "They won't keep it up. They did it for effect."

"She doesn't scream much," I said. "She didn't scream just because they turned a mouse loose in the room."

"No. They hurt her. They probably twisted her arm, but they won't keep on doing it. They have nothing to gain. She doesn't know where we hid the emeralds."

"I don't think I can just sit here much longer."

"We have to wait," he said.

"I'd like to wait while I'm doing something."

"You're cracking," he said. "That's doing something." He walked over to where I stood by the phone. "You may as well memorize this: Either they'll kill her or we'll get her loose, but we can't do that if you crack because she didn't get to take her nightie."

"If I'm cracking, it's because I believe them. I'm impressed. My wife's screams have a certain effect on me. I'd believe them if they said they were going to nominate her Miss Department of Commerce."

"We wait," Padillo said and his voice was like the snap of a whip. "The waiting's part of their pressure. It's hard and they know it's hard and they also know that her screams will make you jumpy about any rescue plan we come up with. But if we don't come up with one, she's dead. And you and I aren't good enough to operate by ourselves. Maybe a few years ago, but not now. We need help. We have to wait for that help."

"We wait," I said.

"All right," he said. "We wait."

I forced myself to mix a drink and turn on the television set and watched a program that asked a panel of scruffy housewives to guess the total cost of a hydroplane, a home printing press and three fonts of type, a case of suntan oil, and a year's supply of cream of potato soup. I guessed $29,458.42. I guessed it aloud, but a woman from Memphis won with a guess of $36,000. I would have liked to have the printing press.

"You watch television much?" Padillo asked.

"Some," I said. "It's like China. If you ignore it, it just gets worse."

Padillo tried pricing the next batch of goodies and placed a poor third, well behind a blonde from Galveston and a grandmother from St. Paul. The grandmother won a motor scooter, some electric stilts that looked interesting, a scholarship to a photography school, a four-foot world globe, and a Japanese sports car. Padillo said he would have liked to have the globe.

The telephone rang and I switched off the set as Padillo answered. It seemed to be long distance and after the operator made sure it was Padillo, she let him say hello. Then he listened. After he was through listening he said: "I'm calling that loan you have with us. I have to call it today." He listened some more and then said: "Good. I'll expect you at this address." He gave the address on Fairmont Street where Hardman's girl friend lived. Then he said goodbye and replaced the phone. "That was Jon Dymec calling from New York. He's at LaGuardia and just missed the shuttle. He'll catch the next one."

Within the next half-hour the phone rang twice and each time Padillo repeated his terse conversation. He didn't have to argue or explain or cajole. All he did was to mention that he was calling the loan.

"Friends of yours?" I asked.

"Hardly."

"Who, then?"

"Agents I have known. Dymec is a Pole and works for Polish intelligence. He's got a UN cover, but spends most of his time in Washington. The girl Magda Shadid works for both Hungary and Syria, and they both probably know it but keep her on because she's inexpensive and they don't have too many secrets that they give a damn about not sharing anyhow. The last one, Philip Price, is British and uses a softdrink company as his cover."

"What's the handle you have on them?"

"I doubled all three of them. They all work for Uncle Sam now."

"And if they don't go along, you'll tattle to their original employers."

"That's it—except that I don't leave myself quite that open. There are the usual envelopes that our lawyer in Bonn would mail. It's old, but it works."

"Didn't he think you were dead? He told me how sorry he was that you were."

"I told him to. I called him from Switzerland."

"He was my lawyer, too," I said.

"He's very discreet, isn't he?"

"The British wouldn't kill Price just because he's a double agent."

"No, but the loss of the fifteen hundred dollars a month we pay him might. If he weren't a British agent, he'd be off the U.S. payroll."

"Any of them know each other?"

"I don't think so, but they may by reputation. They're not amateurs, and the pros in any business get to know the competition."

"They must be very fond of you."

Padillo shrugged and grinned. "They didn't cross over because they had a change of heart. They doubled when I offered them money. It's a soft berth, and they don't want to lose it. That's why I can put the pressure on them like this—once; I'd hate to try it twice."

There was a knock on the door and Padillo went to answer it. It was Mustapha Ali and he and Padillo went through their formal Moslem greeting.

"Man, you sure can rattle it off," Mush said. "How you, Mac?"

"Fine."

"Hard said to carry you over to Betty's. You ready?"

"We're ready," Padillo said. "I just want to put this in the hotel safe." He picked up the leather case that contained the seventeen thousand pounds that he was supposed to earn for not killing Van Zandt and we took the elevator down to the lobby. We found the assistant manager and got the briefcase stored away and then we got in the Buick that Mush drove. It was parked in a tow-away zone, but it didn't have a ticket.

"That TV set in the back along with the phone makes 'em think that the cat who owns this machine would just get a ticket fixed anyhow," Mush said. "It's good as diplomatic plates."

We turned up Seventeenth Street to Massachusetts, went around Scott Circle, and took Rhode Island to Georgia Avenue. The traffic at four-thirty in the afternoon wasn't heavy, and Mush made good time, driving the Buick hard with a lot of skillful use of its power brakes.

"If a man wanted to defend himself in this town," Padillo asked, "what kind of gun could he lay his hands on?"

Mush turned his head to look at Padillo. "You wanna grease gun?"

"Pistol."

"Fancy shooting or close up?"

"Close up."

"Get you a Smith and Wesson .38 belly-gun."

"Can you get two?"

"No trouble."

"How much?"

"Hundred each?"

"They're sold. Now if I wanted to get a knife, what would I do?"

"Switchblade or shakeout?"

"Switchblade."

"You wanna throw it?"

"No."

"I'll get one. Be fifteen dollars."

"You want a switchblade, Mac?" Padillo asked.

"Just make sure it's got a pearl handle," I said. "I've always wanted a pearl-handled one."

"Might not be *real* pearl," Mush said.

"Do the best you can," Padillo said.

Mush let us out in front of the apartment and sped off, presumably in search of our arsenal. We walked up the steps, found Betty's apartment again, and Padillo knocked while I knelt down to unlace my shoes.

"The white rug," I said.

Hardman answered the door in his stocking feet and Padillo knelt down to take off his shoes. "Mush wasn't too early?" Hardman asked.

"Just right," I said.

"They's a good one tonight at Shenandoah Downs in the fourth," he said. "They runnin Trueblue Sue at nine to two."

"With a rhyme like that you can put me down for ten."

"Ten to win," he said and wrote it down in a small blue book.

"You ever win?" Padillo asked.

"I did last spring—or was it winter?"

"You big winner, Mac," Hardman said.

"That means I don't owe him any money."

Betty came in from the bedroom, said hello, glanced at our feet to make sure that the shoes were off, and sailed on into the kitchen.

"I'm sending her to the pictures," Hardman said. "You want me to stick around or disappear?"

"We'd like you to stay," Padillo said.

"Who's comin?"

"Three friends of mine—a Pole, a Hungarian-Syrian, and an Englishman."

"You're not much on matched pairs."

"They were handy and they owe me a favor or two."

Betty marched through again and disappeared into the bedroom. She came out almost immediately wearing a mink stole that looked as if it might still be breathing.

"I need fifty dollars," she told Hardman, planting herself in front of him, her right hand extended. She carried her shoes in her left.

"You just goin to the movies, woman!"

"I might do some shopping."

"Uh-huh," Hardman said, reaching into his pocket and taking out a roll of bills. "You better not do your shoppin in the store that fancy coat's from. Folks there might like to have it back."

"This coat hot?" she said, her voice going from a low contralto to a searing soprano.

"You know it is."

She drew the fur around her and rubbed her chin against the collar. "I'm going to wear it anyhow."

"Here's fifty dollars. You can come on home about nine."

She took the fifty and tucked it in her purse. It seemed to be an easy, practiced gesture. She moved to the door and opened it. "You gonna be here?" she asked Hardman. This time she used a little girl's voice.

"I don't know yet."

"I'd sure like you to, Hard," she said, using the small voice again.

The big man preened a little in front of his male friends. I didn't blame him.

"We'll see," he said. "You just run along now."

"There's a pot of coffee on the stove," she said and left.

We all decided to have coffee and Hardman served it

with quick, efficient movements. "You never knew I used to work the dinin cars on the B&O, did you?"

"I thought you had to be over sixty," Padillo said.

The front door chimes rang before Hardman could tell us about his railroad career. He opened it and a man asked if Mr. Padillo was there. Hardman said yes and the man came in.

"Hello, Dymec," Padillo said. He didn't offer to shake hands.

"Padillo."

"This is Hardman. This is McCorkle."

He nodded at us and glanced around the room. "You mind takin off your shoes?" Hardman said.

The man looked at him without expression. He was about thirty-four or thirty-five, with a face that looked as hard as concrete and had about the same texture and color, except for two patches of red on the high cheekbones. The patches could have been caused by either weather or tuberculosis. I voted for weather; Dymec looked as if he had never been sick in his life.

"Why?" he asked Hardman. The way he said it sounded as if he had been asking why all his life and nobody had ever given him a very good answer.

"The rug, baby. The lady of the house don't want it messed up."

Dymec looked around at the rest of us, saw that our shoes were off, and sat down on a chair and took his off. He wasn't breathing hard when he straightened up.

"How've you been, Dymec?" Padillo asked.

"I heard you were dead."

"Like some coffee?"

Dymec nodded his head, which seemed to have no curves, only corners and planes and lines. He had mouse-colored hair that was cropped close and big ears and small grey eyes. "Cream," he said and his lips barely moved when he spoke.

Hardman served him a cup of coffee and he balanced it on the arm of the chair.

"What do you have going, Padillo?"

"We're waiting for two others. I'm just going to explain it once."

"You've got two too many now."

"Your English is damned near perfect."

"You can call me in this time," Dymec said. "I wouldn't try it again."

Padillo shrugged and leaned back in his chair and pressed his hand against his side. He was due for a change of bandages.

The door chimes sounded again. Hardman was up quickly, moving his weight without effort.

"Mr. Padillo, I believe, is expecting me," another man's voice said.

"Uh-huh. Come on in."

"This is Philip Price," Padillo said when the man was in. "At the door is Hardman. On that chair is Dymec and this is McCorkle. How are you, Price?"

"Well," the man said. "Quite well."

"Do you mind takin off your shoes?" Hardman said. "We're trying to keep the rug nice."

"Hello, Dymec," Price said. "I didn't expect to see you here."

"The shoes, baby," Hardman said.

"I took mine off, Price," Dymec said. "It's as the gentleman said: We're trying to keep the rug nice."

Price knelt and took off his right shoe and put it carefully by a chair. He looked up at Dymec. "Where was the last place we ran into each other? Paris, wasn't it? Something to do with NATO, I believe." He changed his position and knelt on his right leg and took off his left shoe. "The name wasn't Dymec then, was it?"

"And yours wasn't Price."

"True. Well, Padillo, now that you're back from the dead how have you been?"

"Fine. Would you like some coffee?"

"Please. Where would you like me?"

"Any chair," Padillo said. The Englishman took one where he could face the door and keep the rest of us in view. Hardman went into the kitchen and brought him back a cup of coffee. "You want any sugar or cream?"

"Just black, thank you." We sat there and sipped our coffee and looked at each other. The Englishman appeared prosperous. He had on a bluish-grey tweed suit with a white shirt and a dark blue and black tie. The shoes under his chair were black, as were his socks. He had a slim build that looked deceptively frail until you noticed his shoulders. His eyes were brown and their lids seemed to droop over them as if he were only partly awake. I guessed him at around forty-five although there was no grey in the long brown hair that covered the tops of his ears. Maybe he dyed it.

"Seriously," Price said to Padillo, "I heard you were missing and presumed dead. Can't say I went into mourning."

"I just took a little vacation," Padillo said.

"South, I should say, by the tan you're wearing."

"South," Padillo agreed.

"Africa?"

Padillo smiled pleasantly.

"Could it have been you who—"

"West Africa," Dymec said. "I heard about it. Somebody dumped a lot of arms there. A great deal of 7.62 millimeter stuff."

"You always did have an ear for languages, Dymec," Padillo said. "You're talking like an American now. When I first met you, it was more of a Manchester sound."

"He talks good as I do," Hardman said.

Price made a show of looking at his gold wristwatch. "Are we waiting for something or—"

"We're waiting," Padillo said.

We sat there in our stocking feet in the fancy apartment in the northwest section of Washington, D.C., the Negro, the Spanish-Estonian, the Pole, the Englishman, and the Scotch-Irish saloon-keeper, waiting for the Syrian-Hungarian woman to arrive. We sat there and drank the coffee in silence for fifteen minutes before the door chimes rang again.

"I'll get it," Padillo said. He rose and opened the door. "Hello, Maggie, come in."

She came in and the wait had been worth it. She was probably twenty-six or so, and her dark long hair hung carelessly about an oval face whose enormous black eyes swiftly took in everyone in the room. The eyes were complemented by a near-perfect straight nose that just escaped being a shade too long. Her mouth was wide and it was smiling at Padillo. It was a warm, dazzling smile and it looked as if it were used a lot to get a lot of things. She wore a loose coat of soft wool that was woven into large black, white and brown hounds-tooth checks. She said hello to Padillo and turned so that he could take her coat. She wore a white knit dress and her figure was close to perfection. She knew how to stand, how to walk and how to show it all off to its best advantage. Padillo put her coat on a chair.

"May I present Miss Magda Shadid," he said. We all rose. She was worth getting up for. "Mr. McCorkle, Mr. Hardman. Mr. Dymec and Mr. Price."

She nodded at each of us. Then she turned to Padillo and said: "I have something for you, Mike."

"What?"

"This."

She was the only woman I ever saw who slapped a man with her left hand after first feinting with her right.

— NINE —

She should have known better; perhaps she did. Padillo smacked her hard across the cheek with his right palm. It left a bright red mark. She threw her head back and laughed and you could see that her back teeth had no fillings.

"I've been practicing that for two years," she said. "Maybe it will teach you not to stand me up again. I waited for two days in Amsterdam at that ghastly hotel."

"I'm sorry I couldn't keep the date. I'm not sorry I hit you."

"I expected you to hit me," she said rubbing her cheek. "I would have been disappointed if you hadn't. But you didn't have to hit me so hard. Who are all these people?"

"Fellow associates."

"They come in large sizes, don't they?" she said smiling at Hardman. He smiled back. I decided it was just as well that Betty had gone to the movies.

"You don't remember me, do you, Magda?" Dymec said. He still didn't move his lips much when he spoke.

She looked at him and sniffed. "I remember you, but not with pleasure. If I have to remember someone with big, busy hands I'd prefer to remember someone like our sadfaced friend over here." This time she smiled at me. I smiled back.

"You can turn off the charm, Maggie," Padillo said. "We're all impressed."

"Then you can get me a drink, Michael. Scotch-on-the-rocks." She swirled around, as if deciding whom she should do the favor of sitting next to, and chose Price. He nodded at her coolly.

"I'll get the drink," Hardman said. "Anybody else? I got Scotch, bourbon and gin." Everyone chose Scotch.

"When we get our drinks, Padillo," Price said, "could you take stage center and go through your 'I suppose you're all wondering why I've called you here' routine? We are all here, aren't we?"

"You're here because I told you to be here," Padillo said.

Hardman came back from the kitchen carrying three drinks in each hand. He served the woman first and she gave him another smile.

Padillo took a swallow of his and leaned forward. He directed his remarks at Price. "If I had my way, the three of you would be the last I'd ever call in on a deal like this. I don't trust you; I don't like you."

"You like me just a little, don't you, Michael?" Magda said in a sweet small voice.

"I especially like the way you crossed me in Budapest three years ago. I like that so much I sometimes dream about it."

She shrugged and crossed her legs so that we could see them better. They were worth a glance.

"I got you here because I have a handle on each of you and you're all so greedy that you'll do anything to keep on doubling."

The three of them looked at each other. "I say," Price protested, "you're talking a bit freely."

"Am I? Well, I'm going to offer you the chance to form a Mutual-Protective-Association-Against-Michael-Padillo. In other words, I'm going to give you the chance to get off the hook and still keep drawing that fifteen hundred dollars a month from the Crosshatch Corporation. That's where your check comes from every month, doesn't it, Dymec?"

"Mine does," the Pole said, "but it's not fifteen hundred. It's only thirteen hundred."

"Mine's only a thousand," Magda said. Price said nothing.

Padillo grinned and turned to me. "They are greedy, aren't they?"

"What do we have to do to get off the hook, Padillo?" Price asked. "And how will we know that we're really off?"

"By the time you do what you have to do, you'll have enough on me—and on my two friends here—to make us all even. It'll be a standoff. I'll be in no position to inform on you, because you could do the same to me—and to them."

Dymec shook his head slowly. "I would like—as you say—to get off the hook. I don't know about these two, but you wouldn't call me in, Padillo, unless you had a particularly nasty job of work. One that could very easily get me killed."

"You're talking Manchesterese again, Dymec. Maybe I've been too positive. Let me put it this way: If all three of you don't do exactly as I say, I'm going to inform on you and two of you will be dead within a week and Price here might wind up in jail."

"A powerful selling point," Price said.

"I thought you might see it that way."

"Get on with it, Michael," Magda said. "You know you have us or we wouldn't be here. I can't say that I like someone gloating over me."

"Dymec?" Padillo said.

"All right."

"Price?"

"I'll go along."

Padillo nodded. "I'll spell it out for you. You're right, Dymec; I was in West Africa. All over it. When I got to Lomé, a couple of sharpies offered me a sizeable sum to assassinate their Prime Minister."

"Togo doesn't have a Prime Minister," Price said. "It has a President, or did the last I heard."

"You're behind. It's got a general now. But it wasn't Togo; they just made their approach in Togo." Padillo told them the name of the South African country that Van Zandt presided over.

"I'll be damned," Price said.

"How much did they offer you?" Dymec wanted to know.

"Seventy-five thousand, and when I turned them down they said they'd kill me if I didn't shoot Van Zandt when he goes riding down Pennsylvania Avenue next Friday afternoon."

"So you took their money and ran?" Magda said.

"No, I just ran. But they caught up with me and they've

kidnapped McCorkle's wife. If I don't shoot Van Zandt, they kill her. If I go to the police or the FBI, they kill her."

"They'll kill her anyway," Dymec said.

"Of course," Price said.

"What's McCorkle to you?" Magda asked.

"He's my partner. We own a saloon together."

"Was he the one you were using as a cover in Bonn?"

"That's right."

"And now they're getting to you through his wife," she said. "I'm glad you don't like me, Michael. I don't think I want to be a friend of yours."

Padillo ignored her. "Dymec's right. They'll kill her whether I shoot Van Zandt or not. And that's one of the reasons I thought of you. Of all of you. We're going to get her back."

"Do you know where she is?" Price asked.

"No. She was in a house in Georgetown, but they've moved her again by now."

"Do you know who has her?" It was Price asking again.

"No. At least not a list of individuals. But it's probably members of Van Zandt's cabinet."

"What do they propose—a takeover after they dispose of their Prime Minister?" This time Dymec asked the question.

"No," Padillo said. "The whole thing is Van Zandt's idea. He wants to blame the assassination on an American Negro and stir up American public opinion in favor of his country's independence for whites only."

"Colored folks ain't got a chance nowhere," Hardman said in solemn tones.

"They are well treated in Poland," Dymec said.

"That a fact?" Hardman said. He seemed to welcome the information.

"You said it's all Van Zandt's idea," Price said. "What is he—suicide prone?"

"He's eighty-two and he's dying of cancer. He won't be around six weeks from now anyway and he'd just as soon die a martyr for what he thinks is a good cause."

"How do we fit in?" Price asked.

"You help get McCorkle's wife back first."

"What's second?"

"We go ahead with the assassination attempt."

"For the original price, of course," Magda said. "That was seventy-five thousand, wasn't it, darling?"

"That's right, Maggie. Seventy-five big ones."

"And our fee? I assume that you are planning to provide some incentive other than those dreary threats of yours."

"You get five thousand pounds each. Or fourteen thousand dollars."

"That leaves you a tidy profit," Price said. "But not exorbitant. You're getting soft, Padillo."

"You haven't heard it all, Price."

"Let me see whether I have it correct," Dymec said. "We—and I assume that includes all six of us—rescue the woman—McCorkle's wife. Then you agree to go ahead with the assassination attempt for the original fee." He paused and stared at his drink. "It doesn't make sense. Why don't you merely contact the Africans and tell them you've changed your mind? You'll go ahead with the assassination in return for the woman and the fee."

"They'd hold the woman until the assassination was done," Padillo said, "and then they'd kill her. They'd also kill McCorkle and anyone else who they thought knew about it."

"You, too."

"Me, especially. Except that if I killed the Prime Minister, they'd be in no hurry."

"You're not the type to confess," Price said.

"You're leading up to one of your trickier operations, Michael," Magda said. "Usually someone gets hurt. Or dead."

"You'll be well paid for any risk you might take, precious," Padillo said. "But it is a little tricky. It goes like this: the Africans only have this next week in which to get their Prime Minister assassinated in Washington. During this week we are going to have to get Mrs. McCorkle away from them and then we're going to have to work it so that they will hire Dymec here to substitute for me."

"Why me?"

"Because you have the reputation," Padillo said.

"If a larger share is involved, old man," Price said, "I should point out that I have certain qualifications in this line of work."

"They wouldn't go for an Englishman."

"They went for an American," Price said.

"An American who was selling guns on the run, or so they thought."

"I would get a larger share?" Dymec said.

"You'd keep half of what they paid you. You'd split the rest with Magda and Price."

"Your share?"

"Let's just say we've already been paid."

"You're not still working, are you, darling?" Magda asked.

"No. I'm not still working," Padillo said.

"Would the fee still be in the seventy-five-thousand-dollar neighborhood?" Dymec asked.

"Probably."

"And this would be in addition to the fourteen thousand dollars that you have agreed to pay each of us?" Price said.

"Yes. Now is everybody happy about the money? Any more questions about who gets what?"

There were no questions. They sat quietly, not looking at each other. They were probably spending the money.

"When do I do it?" Dymec asked.

"Friday. A week from today."

"Where?"

"Eighteenth and Pennsylvania. A block and a half from the White House."

"Who'll supply the rifle? I have a preference in this line of work, you know."

"It doesn't matter what kind of rifle you have, Dymec," Padillo said. "Because you're not going to kill him. You're going to botch the job and it's all going to come out that it was Van Zandt's idea."

"Good God!" Price said.

Magda smiled brilliantly. "He said it would be tricky, darling."

Dymec nodded. "You sure you're not still working, Padillo?"

"I'm sure."

"It sounds like a typical American intelligence plot," he said. "Only, 2,032 things could go wrong—and probably will."

"You'll get off the hook and you'll be paid," Padillo said. "If it goes really wrong, you'll be fourteen thousand dollars ahead and you'll be rid of me. What more could you want?"

Price licked his lips. "Speaking only for myself, old man, I'd like my full share of that seventy-five thousand."

"When do we get the first payment, Michael?" the woman asked.

"Tomorrow."

"Where?"

"We'll have to find some place else to meet. I'll know by eleven tomorrow morning. Call me at the restaurant's number. What's the number?" he said, turning to me. I told them.

"Who's putting up this fourteen thousand dollars for each of us, if you're not working?"

"You wouldn't know him," Padillo said.

"Will we meet him?"

"No. He's already dead."

— TEN —

"I like your friends," I told Padillo when they had gone. "Maybe we can have them over soon."

"They'd like that," Padillo said. "Just count the silver after you serve the coffee."

"At least they're not squeamish. Dymec seemed a bit miffed when he found out he wouldn't get to shoot anybody."

"Those folks'd do most anything for a dollar, wouldn't they?" Hardman said.

"You're high," Padillo told him. "They'd do it for four bits. That's why we can count on them—up to a point."

"Do you know that point?" I said.

"Sure. It's when they get a better offer from somebody else."

"How about another drink?" Hardman asked. We agreed it would be a good idea and the big man went out to the kitchen to mix them. He came back, carrying the three glasses in one hand.

"Can you find us another place to meet?" Padillo asked him.

"I was just thinking about it. I believe I can get you an office down on Seventh Street—not too far from the main public library."

"That's wino town," I said. "It should be safe."

Padillo shrugged. "As long as it's got a back entrance. Does it?"

Hardman thought for a moment and drew a map in the air to help himself remember. Then he nodded. "It's on the second floor and the stairs lead down to a hall that goes to the front and to the back. The back's an alley."

"Has it got a phone?"

"Unlisted number. We used to count there."

"What happened?" Padillo asked.

"Nothin. We just like to move around."

Padillo put his hand to his side and grimaced. "I'd better get this bandage changed. Any chance of calling that doctor again?"

"Sure. He lives right upstairs. Should be home now." Hardman went over to the pushbutton telephone and hit seven numbers. He talked briefly and hung up. "Be down in a minute," he said.

"What is he, a GP?"

"Something like that," Hardman said.

In five minutes, the door chimes rang and Hardman let in a small, fiftyish man with very dark skin, a wide thick-lipped mouth, and big square teeth that he wore in a friendly grin. He was dressed in a sports shirt, slacks and bedroom slippers and carried a doctor's black bag.

"Hello, Doc. This is Mr. McCorkle and you remember Mr. Padillo from last night. This is Doctor Lambert. He patched you up."

"Hello, there, young fellow," the doctor said. "You're looking a sight better, I'd say. How's the side?"

"It gives me an occasional twinge. Thanks for taking care of it on short notice."

"No bother. You can expect that twinge. But it shouldn't be too bad if it doesn't get infected. A few inches to the right and we'd have had a different story. Where's Betty?"

"Gone to the pictures," Hardman said.

"Let's take a look." Padillo took off his jacket and his shirt. The bandage was of gauze and adhesive tape about six inches below his armpit on his left side. The doctor went into the bathroom, washed his hands, came back and deftly removed the bandage. The cut wasn't over an inch wide, but it was ugly. He cleaned it off, clucked over it, and applied a new bandage. "Not bad," he said. "Not bad at all."

"How's it look?" Padillo said.

"Doing nicely. You can keep that one on for a couple of days. You want something to ease the pain if it acts up?"

Padillo shook his head. "I'm not much on pills."

The doctor sighed. "I wish more of my patients were like that." He looked at Hardman. "Putting on weight, aren't you, big boy?" he said and patted him on the stomach. I sucked in mine before he could prescribe anything. Doctor Lambert went back into the bathroom, washed his hands again, and came back out. He looked at Padillo steadily.

"I don't usually send bills on cases like this."

Padillo nodded. "I didn't think you would. How much?"

"Two hundred dollars. A hundred a call."

"Reasonable. Mac?"

"I'm low. Why don't you pay it, Hard, and put it on my bill?"

The big man nodded, produced his roll again, and pulled off two one-hundred-dollar bills from its insides. He kept the tens and twenties on the outside which spoke well of his modest character, I thought.

The doctor stuck the bills into his pocket, picked up his bag, and turned to Padillo: "I should see you in a couple of days to change it again."

"I'll be back. By the way, do you make house calls?"

The doctor gave him a careful nod. "Sometimes. If it's an emergency."

"You want to give me your phone number?"

"I'll write it down."

"Just say it," Padillo said.

The doctor said it. "You can remember it?"

"I can remember it."

"You have an unusual memory."

"It's a trick. We may have to give you a call in a few days. The patient may be suffering from shock and exhaustion. A doctor may be needed in a hurry. The fee would be high under such conditions, of course."

"Of course," Lambert said.

"Would you be willing to make the call?"

The doctor nodded his head. "Yes, I'd be willing."

"It may be extremely short notice."

"I understand."

"Good. We'll be in touch."

The doctor left and Padillo got dressed. We finished our drinks and were deciding whether to have another when the door chimes sounded again. It was Mush. He was wearing a tan topcoat, dark glasses, and a brown suede hat with a braided band that had a feather stuck in it.

"We'll skip the drink," I said. "We'd better get back to the saloon."

"Mush'll drive you down," Hardman said.

"Good."

"I got what you needed," Mush said.

"What you got?" Hardman asked.

"Couple of blades and a couple of guns." He drew two short-barreled pistols from each of his topcoat pockets and held them loosely in his hands. "They ain't new, but then they ain't old either." He handed one to Padillo, butt first, and one to me in the same fashion. We both checked to see whether they were loaded. They weren't. I looked at the one he handed me. It was a Smith & Wesson .38 Military & Police. The barrel was about an inch long and the butt-stock was rounded and fitted comfortably in my palm. The sights had been removed and if I wanted to shoot anybody from about four inches away, it was a perfect weapon.

Padillo examined his quickly and tucked it into his waistband. It seemed like an uncomfortable place, so I dropped mine into my jacket pocket where I could get to it in five or ten minutes if the occasion arose. A long time ago they had trained me in how to use firearms—all kinds. I had used them and when it was over, I lost interest in guns. I had retained even less interest in knives, which I had also gone to school to learn about.

Mush reached into his topcoat pocket again and produced two switchblades. He gave me the one with the imitation pearl handle. I flicked it open and ran my thumb down its edge, just like a kid in a hardware store. It was sharp. So was the point. I closed it and dropped it into the other pocket of my jacket.

Both Hardman and Mush watched Padillo examine his

knife. It had a plain black case. He tried the spring a half dozen times, watching it carefully.

"Needs tightening," he said. "It's a little slow."

After he tried it for balance and heft he turned to Mush and handed it to him, handle first. "I want to figure out what I did wrong the other night. Try for right under my rib cage. Don't pull it."

Mush just looked at him, and then looked at Hardman as if he needed counsel to make his plea. Hardman cleared his throat. "You want Mush to come at you with this knife?"

"That's right. I want him to go for just under my ribs."

"Uh—Mush is pretty good—" He broke off and looked at me.

"They say he's pretty good," I said to Padillo.

"If he's not, I might break his arm."

Mush shook his head. "You want me to really try?"

"That's right," Padillo said.

"Baby, I can't pull it once I'm started."

"I know."

"Okay. You ready?"

"Ready."

There was no circling about, no feinting, no fancy foot-work. Mush ducked and went in low, the knife flat, its blade horizontal with the floor. He seemed to move incredibly fast. Padillo was faster as he turned his left side to Mush, grasped the knife-holding arm, shoved it away from him, down and back. Mush yelled and flipped to the white carpet. I noticed he had forgotten to take off his shoes.

Padillo reached down and picked up the knife with his left hand and extended his right to Mush. He helped him up. "You're good," Padillo told him.

"What's that trick, baby? Judo?"

"Juarez judo, if there is such a thing."

"You could have kicked my brains out."

"That's the idea."

"How come that cat caught you up in Baltimore?" Mush asked.

Padillo closed the knife and slipped it into a trouser pocket. "You're lucky he did. He's better than you."

Hardman said he would check to find out whether anyone had learned anything about Fredl. He didn't seem hopeful because they would have called if they had. Mush drove us down to the saloon in silence. When he stopped in front, he turned to Padillo and said: "You teach me that, huh?"

"What?"

"That sidestep move."

"Sure, I'll teach it to you." Then he said something in Arabic and Mush grinned delightedly. We got out and the car drove away. "What did you tell him?"

"Chapter four, the Koran: 'Fight for the religion of God.'"

"What was the sideshow for? You didn't have to find out whether you could take him."

"No, but he did. And so did Hardman. We were tossing around some pretty high numbers with my three friends. Hardman wasn't included in for any. I don't know how strong your friendship bonds are, but I'd feel better if he got a cut."

"We're spending the seventeen thousand pounds we got from Underhill on the trio?"

"We'll give them five thousand pounds each. If it makes any difference, it's going for what Underhill wanted. That leaves two thousand pounds for Hardman. Think that's enough?"

"We might have to sweeten it a little."

"I'll take care of it," Padillo said. "I'm going to have to get some funds transferred from Switzerland anyway."

We went through the thick slab door into the restaurant. Business was better than usual for a Friday night, and we moved over to the crowded bar so that Padillo could shake hands with Karl, the bartender.

"You're looking good, Mike," Karl said. "Horst told me you were back."

"So are you, kid. What're you driving?"

"Pre-war Lincoln Continental. Mac found it for me."

"Pretty car. I hear you've chosen Congress as your new hobby."

"It's a howl," Karl said.

"And not as dangerous as woodworking."

"You get the Congressman home O.K. last night?" I asked.

Karl nodded. "I got him to the committee, too, this morning, and then the son-of-a-bitch doublecrossed me and voted wrong."

"How's it look for the redwoods?"

"Not good," he said glumly.

Herr Horst marched up and made us welcome. "You had a call, Herr McCorkle. The person would not leave his name or number. He said to tell you that he was an African acquaintance and that he would call back."

"Send some dinner back to the office for Padillo and me," I said.

"Anything in particular?"

"Use your own judgment. But I'd like a bottle of good wine. What about you?" I asked Padillo.

"Sounds fine."

"Do we have any of that Count Schoenborn 1959 left?"

"Indeed. The *Erbacher Marcobrunn Trockenbeeren-auslese.*"

I nodded and Herr Horst said that he personally would take care of ordering our dinner.

Padillo told Karl that he'd see him later and we went back to the office where I could wait for a phone call and talk to my African friend and perhaps listen to my wife scream again.

— ELEVEN —

After fifteen minutes of waiting the telephone rang and I picked it up.

"This is McCorkle."

"Yes, Mr. McCorkle. Your wife is well and you may talk to her in a few minutes. First, I must tell you of a change in plans. The project that Mr. Padillo is to carry out has been moved to an earlier time: to this coming Tuesday, rather than Friday."

"All right," I said.

"Secondly, the gentleman who is the subject of Mr. Padillo's assignment has expressed a strong interest in meeting him. And you, too."

"Is he in Washington?"

"He flew in this afternoon, earlier than expected. But his appearance before the New York group has also been moved up to Thursday, so it was necessary for us to advance our plans."

"I'd like to talk to my wife."

"Do you understand the changes in times?"

"Yes. When do you want to meet?"

"Tomorrow afternoon."

"Where?"

"At our trade mission. It's on Massachusetts Avenue." He gave me the address.

"All right. What time?"

"Three p.m. Please be punctual."

"Let me talk to my wife."

"Yes, of course."

"Fredl?"

"I'm on, darling."

"Are you all right?"

"Yes, I'm all right. A little tired."

"Did they hurt you?"

"Not badly—just twisted my arm. It wasn't bad."

"And you're all right?"

"Yes, I'm—"

And that was the end of the conversation. I put the phone back and sat down behind the desk. Then I picked it up again and dialed a single number. "Send back a double vodka martini," I said. I looked at Padillo. He nodded. "Make it two doubles."

"Fredl all right?"

"She didn't scream. She said she was all right, but tired. A little tired, she said."

"Was it the same guy on the phone?"

"Yes."

"What did he want?"

"They've advanced the date that you're supposed to shoot Van Zandt. They've set it for this coming Tuesday and we're supposed to meet with them and Van Zandt."

"When?"

"Tomorrow at three o'clock at their trade mission out on Massachusetts."

"You know where it is?"

"I've got the address. I've probably passed it a dozen times, but I don't recall it."

"What does Van Zandt want?"

"He wants to meet the man who's going to kill him."

Padillo rose from the couch and started to pace the small room. There wasn't much space for it—five good steps, and then he had to turn and head back.

"You're not making much headway," I said.

"It's called thinking."

"I'd join you, except that there's not enough room."

There was a knock on the door and I said come in and one of the waiters entered and set the martinis down on the desk. I thanked him and he left.

"Maybe the vodka will help," I said.

"Nothing like a two- or three-martini idea."

"I've had some fine ones on four."

Padillo lighted a cigarette. He inhaled, coughed, and blew most of it out. "You think filters help?"

"I have no idea."

"I quit smoking in Africa."

"For how long?"

"Two days; a little over two days. Three-and-a-half hours over two days to be exact."

"What happened?"

"I admitted I had no will power. It was a great relief."

"I'd say your will power can lick my will power."

"I don't think it would be much of a match."

Padillo quit pacing and sat down on the couch again and absently rolled his cigarette in his fingers. I looked at my martini and then at the desk blotter and then at the filing cabinet. They seemed to be the most interesting objects in the room.

"How did Fredl sound?" Padillo asked.

"I don't know; tired like she said, I suppose."

"You're looking a little frayed."

"I probably look like she feels. I'm worried. It's a new feeling; I never worried about anyone like this before. Maybe it's because I married late. Maybe it's like this when women have babies and men become fathers. For all I know it's part of a giant plot. The world against McCorkle."

"If you'd make it the world against Padillo, I'd go along. It's very tricky, you know."

"What—the world? I agree."

"No. What we have to do tomorrow."

"What?"

"I bow out and get Dymec in."

"Have you thought up a good reason?"

"It's a reason. I wouldn't call it good."

"What do you call it?"

"The FBI."

There was a knock on the door again and this time it was Herr Horst and a waiter. Herr Horst served the *auslese* which we retailed for thirty dollars a bottle, but it was wasted on me. "Try Herr Padillo," I told him. "My palate's gone."

Padillo sampled the wine, pronounced it fit, and Horst skillfully filled our glasses. The waiter served. I don't remember what it was, except that it was hot and the butter was too hard. "Tell Horst that he's serving the butter too hard when you get around to it," I told Padillo.

"We sell much of this?" he asked, holding up his glass of wine.

"Not at thirty dollars a bottle."

"What's it cost us?"

"Nineteen seventy-five a bottle—by the case."

"It's worth it."

"What do we do with the FBI?"

"We use them to bring Dymec in."

"Where do you send off for your ideas?"

"There's no address; just a box number."

I nodded, drank the rest of my wine, shoved my plate back, and lighted a cigarette. It was my fifty-seventh for the day. My mouth had a strange, dark yellow taste. "We were speaking of the FBI—Mr. Hoover and all those polite young accountants and lawyers who work for him. They're on our side now?"

"They will be. For a couple of days anyhow. I'm going to demand protection."

"Protection from whom?"

"I can think of a number of people."

"So can I, but which ones?"

"We'll make it the gun-running crowd."

"A fast set all right. This the African branch?"

"Right."

"And they're after you for what—faulty firing pins or sand in the cosmolene?"

"They don't use cosmolene any more. They've come up with some kind of graphite paste. It comes off easier."

"That's interesting. Probably as interesting as the reason you have for the FBI, provided you have one."

"I'm going to tell them about Angola."

"Ah."

Padillo leaned back on the couch and looked up at the ceiling. "You know much about Angola?"

"It's Portuguese real estate on the West Coast of Africa.

Below the Equator. It's not getting along too well with the Congo."

"That's why I sidetracked the shipment of arms. The already-paid-for shipment."

"Of course."

"They were intended for the mercenaries being trained in Angola and scheduled for the Congo."

"That would never do."

"That's what I thought, I also thought it wouldn't help diplomatic relations between Portugal and the Congo."

"Already strained."

"Exactly," Padillo said.

"Can you string it out?"

"For a few days."

"Who's supposed to be after you?"

"A Portuguese who paid for the guns and trains mercenaries and sends them to the Congo. He's real enough. I almost did some business with him."

"And the FBI's to give you protection against him?"

"His agent—or agents."

"Why?"

"Because in exchange for the protection, I'll tell them about my other arms deals: the ones that did pan out."

"So when Van Zandt asks why you can't do the job, you say the FBI is too interested in you."

"And for proof, all he has to do is look behind me. They'll be there."

"But we have an alternative proposal."

"Dymec. And they can only get Dymec through me and they'll have to guarantee Fredl's safety."

"Some guarantee."

"I can't think of anything better. We'll demand that you

have to talk to Fredl every night between tomorrow and Tuesday. They'll have to allow that or the deal's off."

"We don't have much of a bargaining position."

"No, we don't."

"If the FBI's too close, they're going to tie us in with the assassination attempt. I don't want them around."

"I think we can have them around just long enough to convince the Africans that they're there. That's all we need."

"You're going for the seventy-five thousand dollars?"

"Yes. We'll need it for the trio."

"How do the other two fit in—Price and Shadid?"

"One of them will work with Dymec; the other will work with us when we go after Fredl."

"When we find out where she is."

"We'll find out," Padillo said.

I nodded. "We'd better."

We agreed to meet at ten the next morning and Padillo said he'd like to stay around and watch the place operate. I walked out the front door and turned right. It was almost eleven o'clock. I turned left on Connecticut Avenue and walked up the west side of the street. There weren't too many people abroad and the October weather was cool and dry. The wind blew some litter about the sidewalk. A man in a World War II Eisenhower jacket said he was hungry and I gave him a quarter and wished him luck. He staggered away. I walked on, up Connecticut, towards Dupont Circle. I thought about things I wanted to tell Fredl so that she would laugh and I could listen to her.

But there wasn't any Fredl and there wasn't any laughter and there wasn't anything I could do about it except walk up Connecticut Avenue towards Dupont Circle and listen to the city sounds and the grinding of my teeth. There was no place to go but home; no one to talk to but myself; nothing to do but wait because if I didn't wait, Fredl would exist no more and without her it wasn't much worthwhile. None of it.

I saw them step out of the entrance of the office building. There were three of them. They looked young, about twenty-two or even less. There was some light from a street lamp and I could see their long brown and blonde hair. They wore short zipped-up jackets and tight pants. They had their hands in the pockets of their jackets as they stopped me, one in front, the other two on either side.

"Here's a citizen," the one in front of me said. He was bigger than the other two.

"He's a citizen, all right, Gilly."

Gilly seemed to think that was funny. He laughed and I could see his teeth. He didn't brush them often. Not often enough.

"Excuse me," I said and started around Gilly. He took a hand out of his pocket and placed it against my left shoulder and shoved me back. It wasn't a hard shove.

"You in a hurry?"

"That's right."

"Go ahead and take him, Gilly, he's about your size." This came from the one on my left. He had a small tight mouth and thyroid eyes and a phony drawl.

"You're out late," Gilly said.

"I work late."

"Where do you work, citizen?"

"That's all, son. Get out of my way."

"You're going to fight me, friend."

"I don't want to fight you."

"You're going to fight me," Gilly insisted.

I decided to take out the one with the drawl first. He would be the knife carrier. I hit him with my right fist as hard as I could in the stomach. He whoofed and sat down and threw up. I turned to Gilly and the one who was still standing. Gilly knew enough to throw a left and I tried to go under it but it caught me on the shoulder. The smaller came burrowing in and I kicked him in the kneecap and he danced around holding it. I took the switchblade out of my pocket, flicked it open, and moved towards Gilly. He backed off. He backed until he ran against the building and couldn't go any farther. I took hold of him by the jacket and held the knife up so he could see the blade.

"Which eye do you want to lose, son?"

He closed his eyes and shook his head frantically from side to side. "Don't cut me, mister. For God's sake, don't cut me!" Then he started to cry. I didn't blame him. I let him go. He moved down the side of the building, his back to the wall, and then he ran. The other two ran after him. None of it made any sense; none of it had any purpose. It was just Washington on a Friday night. Maybe it was any city on a Friday night.

There was a group of people standing about twenty feet from me. Three men and two women. A couple of cars had stopped to watch the fight. One of the men detached himself from the group and came over to me.

"There were three of them," he said.

"So there were."

"You carry a knife all the time?"

"Sure," I said. "Don't you?"

"By God, it's a good idea. It sure saved your skin, didn't it?"

I looked down at the knife, closed it, and slipped it into

a pocket. "I had your moral support," I said. "That meant a lot."

I turned and walked to my apartment. I rode the elevator up to the floor where I lived, unlocked the door, took off my coat, fixed a drink, and turned on the television set. I watched Alan Ladd fall through the skylight and get knocked around by William Bendix. It didn't seem to bother him much and I wondered why I was still shaking at two-thirty.

— TWELVE —

I finally fell asleep around six in the morning and awoke at nine-forty-five. The bed was still too large for one person. I got up and went into the kitchen and turned on a burner to heat some water. It was boiling by the time I was dressed. I stirred a cup of coffee and lighted a cigarette, my first for the day. I got the paper from the hall. I called the saloon and told Padillo I was going to be late and he said not to hurry. I didn't. I had another cup of coffee and read the paper. I didn't want to go anywhere.

A front page story told about Van Zandt arriving in Washington early because his UN appearance had been moved up. The story said he would confer with somebody at the State Department, apparently nobody important; meet with members of his consulate and trade mission, and hold a press conference at four p.m., which would be just after he was through going over the details of his assassination. He seemed to have scheduled a full day.

There was a brief item on page twelve about Evelyn

Underhill, fifty-one, who had been struck and killed yes
terday by a hit-and-run driver in the 1100 block of Con
necticut Avenue. There wasn't much else about Underhill

I thought about Padillo's plan to have the FBI traips
around after him so that the Africans would think he wa
too hot and agree to send in Dymec as substitute. Padillo'
reputation would help convince the FBI about his Portu
guese nemesis, at least for a little while. Whether Va
Zandt and his people would buy the package was some
thing else. They were a hard bunch, hard enough to kidna
my wife, hard enough to kill their opposition by runnin
him down in the middle of the afternoon, and hard enoug
to plan an assassination. I decided that they were hard
enough for anything.

I sat there with a cup of cold coffee trying not to thin
of Fredl, and not doing very well at it. So I got up and
rode the elevator down and walked to the saloon. When
arrived, Padillo was saying goodbye on the telephone
"That was Magda," he said. "She's the last to call. We're
to meet them at the Seventh Street address at eleven."

"You'll split the seventeen thousand pounds this morn
ing, right?"

"The fifteen thousand. They get five each."

"Will Hardman be there?"

"No. He says Mush will let us in. We can lock it up
when we leave. We'll keep the key." He glanced at his
watch. "We might as well go."

"All right."

"What did you do, go to bed with a bottle last night?'

"No. Why?"

Padillo eyed me critically. "You look like hell. You look
even worse than you did yesterday."

"I got brushed by some drunk-rollers; three of them."

"Where?"

"About three blocks from here."

"What happened?"

"Nothing. I just showed them my genuine pearl-handled switch blade and they went away."

"Nice neighborhood."

"One of the best," I said. "Wait till you see where we're going this morning."

If Washington has a skid row, the area between Seventh and Ninth is probably it. It runs as far north as N Street; as far south as H. The Carnegie Public Library, located in the middle of a couple of city blocks between Seventh and Ninth, serves as a kind of headquarters for the down-and-out, the drunks, and those who somehow have gone past caring. They can sit in the sun on the curved benches that Andrew Carnegie built in 1899 and read a sign that says the library is intended to be a "University for the People." Most of them look as if they would like a drink.

The library sits in a pleasant enough park with wooden benches and grass and trees and a couple of squirrels. There's a public toilet. In winter one can always go in the library and get warm while nodding over a magazine or newspaper. Across the street from the library on the north side is a deserted seven-story building that once housed a labor union's Washington headquarters until it moved downtown, closer to the White House. There's a church on the west side, a string of bars and secondhand stores on the south, and some liquor stores on the east.

The area is to be included in the city's urban renewal plans someday. In the meantime, the bums sit in the sun and wonder where the next bottle of wine is coming from and read the stone letters above the library entrance which proclaim that the whole thing is "Dedicated to the Diffusion of Knowledge."

Hardman had his sometime collection office around the corner a block or so from the library on Seventh. We climbed a flight of stairs and Mush was there, leaning against the door. He and Padillo said something in Arabic to each other. Then Mush opened the door and handed me the key. "Hard says keep it as long as you need it."

"Thanks."

"Need anything, he say, just holler. You got his car telephone number."

"I've got it," I said.

"He'll be cruisin today."

"Tell him we'll see him later."

Mush nodded and went down the stairs two at a time. We went into the one-room office. The window that faced Seventh looked as if it hadn't been opened or washed since Roosevelt was sworn in for his second term. There was a yellow oak desk with a telephone on it and a blotter that had accumulated a thick coating of dust. There were six chairs, the metal kind that fold and can be stacked against the wall. There was no name on the pebble-glass door; no carpet on the pine floor. It was an office that would be rented to somebody who sold penny stocks, or who promoted Lonely Hearts' club, or who founded organizations to hate someone or abolish something. It was an office that seemed to have witnessed scores of failures and a half-a-hundred shattered dreams. It was an end-of-the-line office, and Hardman sometimes used it as a numbers counting house and sometimes lent it to friends who wanted a place to split up forty-two thousand dollars among three thieves.

Philip Price arrived first. He said hello and looked around

the office, dusted off a chair, and sat down. "Am I early?" he asked.

"You're on time," Padillo said.

"Good."

We waited five minutes and Dymec arrived. He sat down without bothering to dust off anything. I don't think he noticed the office.

Magda Shadid arrived three minutes or so after Dymec. She wore a loose, white wool coat and brown alligator shoes with wicked heels.

"It's so dirty," she said. Padillo gave her a handkerchief.

"Clean off a chair," he said.

"I'll get my coat just filthy."

"Is this all?" Price asked.

"This is all," Padillo said.

"Where's the nigger?"

"He's busy."

"On the job?"

"On something else."

"Today we get money, right?" Dymec said.

"Today you get money," Padillo said. "First you get some information. Can you wait?"

"Looks as if we'll have to," Price said.

"McCorkle and I are meeting with Van Zandt and his people, whoever they are, this afternoon."

"I saw in the paper that he flew in early," Price said.

"Why does he want to meet you?" Magda said. "You're going to kill him, or you're supposed to."

"We didn't ask," I said. "We're not in much of an asking position. If he wants to see us, we want to see him. All we've had up until now are a couple of phone calls and a note."

"We see him at three o'clock this afternoon," Padillo said. "I'm going to name Dymec as my substitute then."

"What reason will you give?" Dymec said.

"Would I normally tell you?"

Dymec thought a moment. "No. You wouldn't. You'd only mention money to me."

"Then you don't need to know my reason."

"Agreed."

"They'll probably want to check on you. Can they?"

"I have a certain reputation, not under the name Dymec, of course, but—"

"I'll mention another name."

He nodded.

"They'll probably want to meet you, possibly tonight, possibly tomorrow. Keep yourself available."

"Of course."

"What about us two?" Price asked.

"You'll work with Dymec after he's given the assignment. Don't forget; the idea is to blow it, not to make it come off. I'll tell you what I have in mind later."

"And me?" Magda said.

"You'll be with McCorkle and me. You'll help us get Mrs. McCorkle out from wherever she is. A woman will probably come in handy."

"I will still get my full share, won't I, Michael?"

"Yes."

"So all we have to do is lay about and count our money until you call?" Price said.

"That's it."

"When will we meet again?" Price asked.

"Tomorrow. Here at the same time."

"That will be Sunday."

"That's right."

Padillo opened the briefcase that had once belonged to Underhill and put three stacks of pound notes on the dusty table. "It's all there," he said, "five thousand pounds each. You don't mind if we don't hang around while you count it?"

Magda had already picked up her stack and was thumbing it quickly. "Call me at the saloon about five-thirty, Dymec," Padillo told him. The angular man nodded, but said nothing as he kept on counting his pile of bills, moving his lips silently as he did so. "Close the door when you leave," Padillo said. This time Price nodded and went on counting his money.

"Let's go," Padillo said. We went down the steps and out the back door into an alley. We walked down to I Street and then to Ninth and caught a cab that drove us back to the saloon.

"We should have another caller soon," Padillo said.

"Who?"

"Somebody who will want to find out what happened to Underhill and the seventeen thousand pounds he was carrying."

We opened the thick slab door and walked towards the back. We checked with Herr Horst, made a few suggestions, okayed five purchase orders, and took a quick look at Friday's receipts.

"We must be the richest kids on the block," Padillo said.

"It was a typically better-than-average day. Fortunately, the average keeps rising."

We went back into the office. "Someone call you about Underhill?"

"No. But by this time they know he's dead and they may have had somebody bird-dogging Van Zandt."

"If you're right, we'll be their next stop."

"What should we tell them?" he asked.

"Will it be a them or a him?"

"I have no idea. Probably a him; I doubt that they have enough money to send more than one."

"Maybe it will be his wife."

"That's all we need."

Padillo picked up the telephone and dialed a number. I just listened. I didn't really much care whom he called.

"Mr. Iker," he said.

I could hear Iker answer over the telephone, but I couldn't understand the words.

"This is Michael Padillo; I'd like to talk to you." Iker's voice made some more noise. "About the business we discussed in my hotel room." Padillo listened again, then he said; "Whenever an attempt is made on my life, I often change my mind." Iker's voice went up a few notches. "I don't bluff, Iker. Be in the lobby of my hotel at six o'clock. We'll go up to my room and I'll show you my stab wound." He hung up.

"I wonder if the Wise Lady from Philadelphia is still around?" I said.

"Who?"

"There was once this family who put salt instead of sugar into a cup of tea. Their name was Peterkin, as I remember. So they went to the doctor and the pharmacist and the grocer and God knows who all, trying to make the salt taste like sugar. Nothing worked. Finally they went to the Wise Lady from Philadelphia."

"And?"

"She told them what to do."

"What?"

"Pour a new cup of tea."

Padillo leaned back in his chair and put his feet on the desk and looked up at the ceiling. "You don't remember her name, do you? If you do, we'll give her a call."

— THIRTEEN —

About a quarter after two we walked over to my apartment building and got my car out of the basement garage. Padillo glanced at the mileage on the speedometer.

"You don't use it much."

"We take long drives on Sunday."

"Then you really need something that will do one-fifty."

"That's what I thought."

I turned down Twentieth Street and then left on Massachusetts. We went past the Cosmos Club, around Sheridan Circle, and past the Iranian Embassy. The trade mission was located in a narrow four-storied house that had been converted into office space. It was flanked by similar houses that served as embassies for a couple of small South American countries. There were a half-dozen Cadillacs parked in no-parking zones and it only took us fifteen minutes to find a place to put the Corvette.

We walked a block back to the trade mission that had the solid, respectable appearance of a rich man's house

He flushed and looked at Van Zandt. The old man put his hands flat on the table, raised his elbows until they were level with his shoulders, and leaned forward. He looked like an angry turkey buzzard about to take off. His hands had brown mottled spots on their backs.

"We are not here to squabble," he roared. "We are here to plan my death and I damn well intend to see that it's planned correctly."

"Sorry, sir," Boggs said.

Darragh, the Minister of Home Affairs, looked at Padillo. "Are you willing to proceed?"

"With what?" Padillo asked.

"With the discussion."

Padillo leaned back in his chair, produced a cigarette, lighted it, and blew the smoke out. "Sure," he said. "I'll discuss it. It's set for Tuesday now, I understand."

"That's correct," the old man said. "That gives me a little less than three days of living left, doesn't it?" He seemed to almost enjoy the thought.

The two younger men stirred uncomfortably in their chairs. "How does it feel to plan a man's death like this, Mr. Padillo?" Van Zandt said. "I mean in a civilized manner, over the coffee and cigars that I'll offer later? I understand you've done this type of work before."

"So they say."

"I remarked that look about you. You've got the hunter's eye. At eighty-two I'm not sorry for a damned thing so I'm not sorry about ending this way. Tell me, what type of piece do you plan to use?"

"I hadn't thought about it. What would you say to a Garand M-1—the old World War II standby?"

"No sporting piece for you?"

"It depends upon what's available. I have no favorites."

The old man leaned back in his chair. "Just recalling my first military rifle. Was an old Lee Metford Mark II with a ten-round magazine and a half-length cleaning rod attached. Damned thing weighed more than ten pounds, and it stood more than four feet tall."

Van Zandt stopped talking and coughed. It was a deep, wracking cough. His face flushed and a vein popped out on his forehead. He shook his head when he was done.

"Let's get on with it," he said. "First, let me say it's a dirty business. I know it and you gentlemen know it. Kidnapping a man's wife—well, it's something that I'd rather have had no part of. But it's done; it's done. I'm going to have myself assassinated because of politics, but that's usually the reason for assassinations, isn't it? Unless you have one that's wasted, like that fool Verwoerd's. The only thing he ever drew were madmen. He could have died for something, if he'd planned it. I'm dying anyway, you know. Be gone in a month or two, no matter what. Cancer of the stomach. Nasty thing—a truly nasty thing." The old man paused and stared across the room. He seemed to be staring at nothing. The two younger men twitched in their chairs.

"Just remembering," Van Zandt said. He smoothed his long thin white hair with a mottled hand. "Remembering how it was sixty years ago before they built the roads and brought in their stinking autos and spread out their filthy cities. It was a good country then. Still a good country and that's what my dying's all about. To keep it a good country."

He looked at me. "You have blacks here and you have trouble with them, don't you, Mr. McCorkle?"

"We have all kinds of trouble," I said. "We've got a big country."

"Have you found a solution to your color problem? Have you? Of course not. Never will either. Black and white can't live together. Never could and never will. That's why I'm dying. My death will slow down the blacks. It won't stop them. I know that. But it will slow them down. It will shock people."

"Nobody grieved much over Verwoerd," Padillo said.

"Of course not. The bloody fool got killed in his own country, by a madman and white at that. My country wants to be independent and run its own affairs, elect its own government, conduct its own foreign relations, arrange its own trade agreements. The blacks can't do this—they haven't a notion."

He stopped again and again the young men twitched. "My death will help do this one thing, gentlemen: it will slow down the encroachment of the blacks on the affairs of my country. It will create sympathy. It will—since I am to be assassinated in the United States—weaken your country's resistance to our independence. My death at the hands of a black will give my country twenty years to put its affairs in order. By then it will be able to cope. I assure you: we will be able to cope. Rhodesia, South Africa, and us—we will conduct our own affairs. And my death will serve this purpose." He paused again. "Separate development," he said firmly. "It's the only solution. Your country should adopt it."

Padillo moved his chair closer to the table. "I don't know if your death will affect the future of your country or not. It sounds to me as if you're giving it too much weight. Maybe it will create the political climate you're looking for and get the British off your back. Maybe they'll let you go independent and then a hundred-thousand whites can go on keeping two million blacks in their place—

wherever their place is. The back door, I suppose. Maybe it will work; maybe it won't. But before you get too carried away with it all, let me mention something. I won't be the one who pulls the trigger."

There was a brief silence. The old man looked at Padillo and then at Boggs and Darragh. It was Darragh who sighed as he spoke.

"I don't like to keep mentioning Mrs. McCorkle, but—"

"You don't have to mention her," Padillo said. "I only said that *I* couldn't do it. I didn't say it couldn't still be done."

"Why can't you do it, Mr. Padillo?" Van Zandt asked.

"Because the FBI is interested in me. They're interested in the guns I ran in Africa. They've had a tail on me since I've been here."

"We've been watching you, too, Padillo," Boggs said. "We haven't noticed the tail, as you say."

"Then you haven't looked. We shook them off to come here. But that will only make them interested. They'll make sure they stick next time."

"Obviously you couldn't carry out your assignment if you are under strict surveillance," Van Zandt said. "But how do we know that you are?"

"I'll be back at my hotel at six tonight," Padillo said. "Just have someone in the lobby. There'll be at least two from the FBI there; perhaps more. They're not hard to spot."

"Someone will be there, Mr. Padillo," Darragh said. "I can assure you."

"You can also be there at six in the morning. They'll be there then, too."

Van Zandt shook his head. "I don't like this, Wendell. I don't like to have plans go wrong."

"They haven't necessarily gone wrong," Padillo said. "The assassination can still be brought off."

"By whom?"

"By a professional."

There was another silence and then the old man went into another coughing fit.

"How could we trust him?" he said between coughs.

"You engage me as the contractor. I just subcontract it out. The chief difference is that I'll have to have the seventy-five thousand dollars you mentioned in Lomé. The man I have in mind doesn't come cheap."

"Our hold on you would still be Mrs. McCorkle?"

"With one exception. McCorkle must be allowed to talk to her at length Monday night. He must also be allowed to talk to her just prior to the assassination."

"You don't seem to trust us, Mr. Padillo," Van Zandt said.

"I don't trust you at all. I think you're desperate and I think you're scared. When you killed Underhill, you showed how desperate you are. You're also sloppy. Boggs here talks to his wife who talks to her sister who is Underhill's wife. This is supposed to be a conspiracy. I agree with McCorkle. It's becoming a convention."

"We have taken steps to make sure that Mrs. Boggs doesn't talk to anyone else," Boggs said.

"I'll bet you have," Padillo said. "But you do things after the fact. When this is over, there'll still be McCorkle and his wife and me around. We'll know what happened. What do you plan to do with us?"

Darragh spread his hands in an open gesture. "You'll have become involved, Mr. Padillo. You were to have been the killer; now you'll be an accessory. So will Mr. McCorkle."

"And his wife?"

"I doubt that she would jeopardize her husband."

"This fellow you say you know. Who is he?" Van Zandt asked.

"He's a professional."

"Does he have a name?"

"He has several."

Van Zandt stared at Darragh. "I don't like things to go wrong, Lewis. And things have gone wrong. Now we must employ yet another person. We have endangered the entire plan."

"Perhaps not," Darragh said smoothly. "We would like to meet this professional, as you call him, Mr. McCorkle. Can that be arranged?"

"Yes."

"Today?"

"Probably."

"And could you give us a name that he has used so that we might determine his qualifications?"

"The name would depend upon what country you planned to make your inquiry in."

"Spain? Madrid, perhaps."

"Ask about a man who called himself Vladisla Smolkski there in 1961."

Darragh asked how it was spelled and Padillo told him. "We will send a cable to our representative there at once. We should have an immediate answer. If it is satisfactory, we wish to meet this man."

"He'll be available."

"How shall we contact you?"

"Call either McCorkle or myself. The meeting will be

set up for an office on Seventh Street." He gave them the address and Darragh wrote it down next to Dymec's other name.

"I suggest that you bring money," Padillo said.

"I don't think we would like to pay all at once," Boggs said.

"Just half. And you pay it to me, not to the man you meet."

Van Zandt chuckled. "You intend to make a profit from my death, Mr. Padillo."

"Just covering expenses. I may have to take a long trip when this is over."

"Do you feel that you can bring it off successfully?" Van Zandt asked.

"It shouldn't be too hard. You won't have much protection, if any. The United States doesn't seem to think you're important enough."

"It should stir the world," the old man said. Darragh and Boggs squirmed some more in their chairs. Van Zandt's flights seemed to embarrass them.

"We'll make definite plans tonight," Boggs said.

"The exact time, the place, everything," Padillo said. "There's just one more thing."

"What?" Boggs said.

"Mrs. McCorkle. I suggest that you make sure that she is returned unharmed after this is over."

"We intend to keep our bargain," Boggs said.

Padillo stood up. "I'm glad that you do," he said, "because you wouldn't live long enough to regret that you didn't."

— FOURTEEN —

B oggs and Darragh followed us out into the hall when we left. Van Zandt continued to sit at the large carved desk, his pale green eyes gazing out from under the white forest of his eyebrows. He wasn't watching us leave. He may have been looking at his country as it was sixty years ago, before the automobiles and the airplanes and the Coca-Cola. Or he may have been deciding whether to take a pill to kill the pain.

"Don't threaten us, Padillo," Boggs said when the sliding doors were closed.

"I wasn't threatening you. I was just describing what was going to happen if Fredl McCorkle isn't returned safely. You tried to buy me and you tried to frighten me and neither worked, so you pressured me through another person. That was a mistake on your part."

"Then you also have the irate husband to consider," I said. "You've convinced me that you might kill her if I went to the police, or if the assassinaton doesn't come off.

I'll put up with all of that. I might even put up with a little more, just to make sure she's all right. But not much more. Especially, not as much as having her scream over the telephone at me. That was another mistake you made."

Boggs looked around to see who was listening. There was nobody.

"How much do you think we have riding on this, Jocko?" His voice was low and fast. He seemed furious, and a flush started rising from his collar-line. By the time it reached his ears, it was a bright pink. "We're not playing for coppers, we're playing for an entire country and the death of that old man in there is the winning ticket. If he's not killed next Tuesday, then Darragh and I and a half-dozen other chaps may as well pack it in." He was talking so fast that a trace of spittle formed at the corner of his mouth. Darragh nodded his dark head in agreement. His mouth was turned down at the corners.

"We don't give a damn about what you feel or think or threaten," Boggs went on. "You're nothing and your woman's nothing. You're just a trigger finger to us and that trigger finger had better work when it's supposed to."

We were standing in the hall, the pair of them facing the pair of us. Darragh hunched his shoulders and leaned forward and his voice was as low and as fast as Boggs's. "You mean as much to us as a couple of niggers, and nothing means less than that."

Padillo looked first at Boggs and then at Darragh. "Is that all?" he asked.

Boggs took a handkerchief from his pocket and wiped the corners of his mouth. He was still pink. He nodded his head. "Could I say it more plainly?"

"No," Padillo said. "You couldn't." He turned to me. "I take it you understand the gentlemen?"

"We don't mean much to them," I said.

"Well," Padillo said, and smiled brightly at them, "it was nice talking to you."

The flush started rising again on Boggs's neck. "Have that man available, Padillo."

"Sure," he said, and smiled again. "Let's go."

We left the four-story house and walked towards the car.

"We didn't seem to do too well playing the heavies," I said.

"It was a draw," Padillo said. "Although they had better lines."

I made a U-turn on Massachusetts and started back toward downtown. I drove quickly, darting through traffic, and taking a couple of chances on two women drivers who thought that twenty miles an hour was reasonable haste. Padillo turned around and looked out the rear window.

"The green Chevrolet?" he asked.

"Uh-huh."

"A girl's driving."

"She was parked up the street from the trade mission."

"Don't lose her," Padillo said.

"I just wanted to make sure that she knew who we were."

"Let's talk to her."

"Where?"

"You have any ideas?"

I thought a moment. "Rock Creek Park. The trees are just turning."

"It should be pleasant."

I turned right at Waterside Drive and the green Chevrolet followed. I drove through Rock Creek Park until I came to the first spot that had picnic tables, shifted down into second, and turned in. The Chevrolet shot past, stopped, then backed up. Padillo and I got out of the car. The Chevrolet pulled into the parking place. The girl behind the wheel cut the engine and sat in the car looking at us. Then she opened the door and got out.

She was a brown-eyed blonde and her hair was cut short so that it seemed to form a helmet over her head. She walked toward us slowly, one hand in the deep leather purse that she had slung over her right shoulder. She wore a brown tweed coat and a beige skirt. She had long slim legs and the dark brown pumps she wore picked their way carefully through the gravel of the parking lot. Her brown eyes rested first on my face and then on Padillo's and then back on mine. The eyes were wide and they seemed a little frightened. She was all of twenty-one.

"Which one of you is Michael Padillo?" she asked, and her lower lip trembled a little when she said it. Her voice was soft and low and it sounded reminiscent of another voice I had heard before.

"If you plan to shoot him with that gun you have in your purse," Padillo said, "he's not here." As he talked he moved to his right. I moved to my left. The girl's eyes tried to keep us both in sight, but we were too far apart.

"Damn," she said, "damn, damn, damn." Then she took her hand out of her purse. "All right," she said. "No gun."

"You didn't really want to shoot me anyhow. I'm Michael Padillo."

"What happened to my father?"

"Do I know your father?"

"He came here to see you and now he's dead."

"Your name is Underhill then."

"Sylvia Underhill."

"Your father was run down by a car."

"They told me that," she said. "They told me the car didn't stop."

"That's right," Padillo said. "It didn't stop."

"Why didn't it stop?"

"This is Mr. McCorkle, Miss Underhill."

She looked at me. "He mentioned your name, too."

"I met him briefly."

"I flew all night and all day," she said. "May I sit down?"

We sat on the wooden benches of the picnic table and the girl looked around as if she realized for the first time that she had traveled twelve thousand miles and wanted to find out if the tour was all that the travel agent had said it would be.

"It's nice here," she said. "This is a beautiful park."

"Would you like a drink?" Padillo asked.

"A drink?"

"What do we have?" he asked me.

"The emergency ration in the rear. Brandy."

"Brandy?" he asked her.

"That would be fine, thank you."

I got the bottle of brandy out of the car and three small plastic cups. It was cool under the trees, almost chilly in the mid-October afternoon, and the brandy tasted warm and reassuring to me. But then it always did.

"How did you know us?" Padillo asked.

"I guessed. I arrived this morning and saw the police and went to your restaurant this afternoon. They said you had gone so I asked what kind of auto you drove. I didn't know where else to go so I drove to the trade mission. I saw a car that could have been yours. I waited. When you came out, I followed."

"Do you know why your father wanted to see me?" Padillo said.

She nodded her head. "Yes. Did he get the chance to tell you?"

"Yes; he did."

She paused and looked around and then she looked down into her plastic cup. "Did you agree?" She seemed to hold her breath after she said it.

Padillo looked at me. I nodded slightly. "Yes. We agreed."

Her breath came out in a soft sigh. "I'm afraid I don't have the money—it wasn't with his things, they said."

"We have the money."

Her shoulders slumped in relief and she drank the rest of the brandy. "I wasn't really sure what I was going to do. I was frantic when we heard about Dad and then they called the meeting and decided that I would have to go."

"Who called a meeting?" I asked.

"They're just people who believed as Dad did. Some farmers, some professors, a few lawyers and doctors and—well—just people. Some of them were in the parliament with Dad. They're not organized. They're not even the kind to form an organization. They're just people who don't agree with Van Zandt, who hate what he's trying to do."

"And they appointed you to take your father's place?" Padillo asked.

"There was no choice. Most of them couldn't get exit visas on such short notice. I could—or Mother could—because of Dad's death. Somebody had to come. There just wasn't anyone else."

"How old are you?" Padillo said.

She looked at him. "I'm twenty-one."

"What were you going to do if I hadn't agreed to go along with your father's suggestion?"

"Anything that would be necessary to make you change your mind, Mr. Padillo," she said. "Anything."

"You're awfully young for anything."

"Perhaps that would be an advantage."

He nodded. "You're not as young as I thought."

She took a cigarette from her purse and I lighted it for her. It didn't make her look any older. "Could you tell me about it?" she asked.

"How much do you know?"

"I know that Dad came here to see you after he found out about you. I know that he and the rest of them raised seventeen thousand pounds. It was all they could raise. They're not very popular and business has been bad for some. He was going to offer you the seventeen thousand to expose the plot—to make sure that Van Zandt wasn't killed."

"They have Mr. McCorkle's wife," Padillo said. "They say they'll kill her if the assassination doesn't come off."

The girl looked at me and her eyes were wide. "That's terrible. That's incredible."

He looked at his watch. It was five-twenty. "Where are you staying?"

"I'm not staying anywhere. I went to the police and then I went to your restaurant and then I rented the car and came here."

"We'd better make it some place safe," I said.

"Your place?"

I nodded.

"I couldn't—"

Padillo cut her off short. "He's harmless. He's in love with his wife."

"If you whistle at breakfast, the deal's off," I said.

She smiled. It made her look about six years old at Christmas. "I'm sorry I objected. It wasn't that, it was— I'll promise not to whistle."

Padillo looked at his watch. "I have an appointment at six."

"Take my car," I said. "We'll go in hers." I unclipped the ignition key from my ring and gave it to Padillo. "How long do you think it will take?"

"An hour; maybe two. It depends upon how well I lie."

"Call me at the apartment. We'll have dinner."

"Good."

Padillo got in the Corvette and drove off. I gathered up the cups and the brandy bottle. "Can you put these in that purse of yours along with the gun?"

"It's a very small gun."

"Nothing worries me more than a small gun, unless it's an unloaded one."

She wanted me to drive so I did. We came out on P Street and I drove east.

"Will you tell me about it, please?" she finally asked. "About all of it? I'm terribly sorry about your wife, but I have to know what Dad was doing when he died. I have to know if it makes any sense."

"I can tell you about that right now," I said as I turned into the basement garage. "None of it makes any sense."

I got her suitcase out of the back seat and we took the elevator up to my apartment. I showed her the guestroom and bath and said that I would be in the livingroom. She came in a few moments later, looking a little less tired, or maybe she had done something to her face. She was an extremely pretty girl and without her topcoat the rest of her complemented her long slender legs. I asked her if she wanted a drink and she said no, she would like a cup of coffee so I went into the kitchen and heated the water and smoked a cigarette while I waited for it to boil. There was a coffeepot some place, but we never used it. Fredl had grown up on black-market American instant coffee and she insisted it was better than the ground variety. It was one of the major compromises of our marriage.

After Sylvia Underhill took her first sip of coffee I told her about what had happened to her father and what he had wanted us to do.

"And you agreed to do it?"

"Yes."

"But after he was dead, you didn't have to."

"That's right."

"You could have kept the money and just forgotten about it."

"We could have kept the money," I said.

"He wasn't cut out for this," she said.

"Few people are."

"Are you?"

"No."

"Is Mr. Padillo?"

"He's had practice."

"He seems a strange man. I read the dossier that my father got some place. Has he really done what it says— I mean, all of those things?"

"I haven't seen the dossier, but Padillo has had what could be called a full life."

"You've known him a long time, haven't you?"

"Yes."

"I don't think I would ever know what he was really thinking. Does he do all these things because he believes in them or because he enjoys doing them or why?"

I looked at my watch. It was six-thirty. It seemed time for the cocktail hour. "You sure you wouldn't like a drink?"

"No thank you."

"I think I'll have one."

"All right."

I walked over to the bar and mixed a vodka martini. "Padillo has had one ambition in life from the time he was sixteen years old, and that is to run a nice quiet saloon. It's something that we have in common. But he was born with three handicaps for a saloon-keeper: an extremely quick mind, an unusual gift for languages, and superb muscular control—far better than most athletes. He didn't work at any of these; they just happened to him, just as you happened to turn out to be an extremely pretty girl.

"Some people found out that all these handicaps were wrapped up in one man, so they used them—much as they would use a lawyer or a surgeon. When they learned that something was wrong somewhere, they would send Padillo in to fix it. He did it not because he wanted to do it, but because it was the price he paid for being allowed to do what he really wanted, and that's to run a saloon. He would have liked to have run one in Los Angeles, but it never worked out."

"When you speak of some people, you're talking about your government."

"No. I'm speaking about some people. They work for the government and they're caught up in their ambitions and their convictions and the power of decision and command that they've acquired. They would use Padillo to fix things that they thought needed fixing."

"He killed people, the dossier said."

"I suppose he did."

"Because these people in government told him to?"

"Yes."

"Were they always right?"

"Probably not."

"Then he killed innocent people?"

"He killed people who were very much like himself, I'd say—as innocent or as guilty. They were chosen to die because somebody in our government thought that the world would be a better place to live if they weren't around any more. Perhaps they thought it would make a difference, and maybe the world did get better for them because they received a promotion or a discreet commendation. But it didn't change things much for the rest of us."

"And it was someone like that in my country's government who decided that my father should die."

"Probably. They wrapped it up in patriotism, their own brand, and tied it up with their own convictions, and your father was killed. Those who killed him considered it progress. For you it's a senseless tragedy because your father's death seems meaningless. Most deaths are."

"But Van Zandt's death would have a purpose."

"He thinks so and so do those who support him. He thinks it will change history and give him a share of immortality. Those who support him think it will make the world a better place to live—for them."

"There's something that bothers me," she said. "Why are you going to do what my father asked you to do? Why don't you just do what they wanted you to do and get your wife back and then just forget about it? You seem to be able to take death so very casually."

"How long do you think they would let my wife live after it was over?"

"I don't know. Would they kill her?"

"I think so."

"What are you going to do?"

"Try to get her back."

"And if you don't?"

"I don't know," I said. "I haven't thought about that yet. I don't think that I can."

— FIFTEEN —

Karl didn't flick an eye when I walked in with Sylvia
Underhill on my arm. It was that kind of place. We
took a broad view of everything.

"Padillo here yet?"

"He's in back."

"Call him and tell him I'm here. Which table?"

"Thirty-two, in the corner," Karl said. "Drinks?"

"We'll wait for Padillo."

We followed one of the waiters over to the table that I
had asked to be reserved after Padillo had called me from
his hotel. The waiter helped Sylvia with her chair and
hovered around a bit more than usual because she was with
the owner. Padillo came out from the back and crossed
the room quickly, counting the house as he came. We were
full and those without reservations were lining up at the
bar. The customers liked the bar for its generous drinks,
its fast service and Karl's knowledgeable gossip about
Washington. He served a quick, bright line of chatter that

just bordered on slander. It provided an interesting contrast to Herr Horst's meticulously correct formality.

"How'd it go?" I asked after Padillo was seated and had said hello to Sylvia.

"I didn't remember how well I can lie."

"They went along?"

"Take a look at the bar—the third and fourth seats from the end."

I waited a few moments and then looked around, as if for a waiter. Two men in their early thirties sat at the bar, half-turned to the room, trying to look unremarkable. They succeeded. Each had a bottle of beer and a half-full glass at his elbow. They didn't seem thirsty or worried about the beer going flat.

"The two nursing the beer?" I asked.

"They picked me up at the hotel when I left."

"Who are they?" Sylvia asked.

"They're from the FBI."

"They followed you?"

"Yes."

"Why?"

"Because they think I'm in danger."

"What happened when you got to the hotel?" I said.

"You think we could get a drink?" Padillo asked.

I held up a hand and waved it slightly. A waiter materialized. We ordered three vodka martinis.

"You recall that circular seat that the hotel has around the fountain in the middle of the lobby?" Padillo said.

"Yes."

"When I arrived at six, Iker and Weinriter were sitting on it, waiting for me. They didn't make it too obvious, but it was obvious enough. Darragh was sitting on the other side of the thing. He followed us to the elevator."

"You should have invited him up."

"He still looked unhappy."

"Are you speaking of Lewis Darragh?" Sylvia said.

"Yes."

"I'm not sure what you're talking about."

"You tell her," I said. "I've been talking all evening about how clever you are."

Padillo sketched it quickly—how we needed the FBI surveillance to convince Van Zandt that Dymec should be brought in as the substitute assassin.

"You told Weinriter and Iker about Angola?" I asked.

"I even drew them a map, an accurate one."

"They look at your side?"

"Iker wanted to. He also wanted to know who the doctor was."

"And they bought the whole thing?"

"Reluctantly. They still want to hear about the arms deals that did take place."

"That's next week, I take it."

"Possibly the week after."

The waiter brought the martinis. I told him we would order in ten minutes.

"Now that you have your Federal guardians, what do you plan to do with them?"

"I don't know. It's supposed to be a twenty-four-hour surveillance."

"They can't keep that up forever."

"I probably told the story too well. I'll try to think up another one that will get them to fade out tomorrow."

Herr Horst came over and Padillo introduced him to Sylvia Underhill. He recommended the tournedos and a wine from the Ahr and we agreed to try them after another martini. A waiter brought a telephone over and plugged it into the jack. "It's for you, Mr. McCorkle," he said.

I picked it up and said yes.

"We'll accept the substitute, McCorkle." It was Boggs's voice. "But we want to talk to him."

"When?"

"Tonight?"

"I'm not sure we can reach him tonight. I want to talk to my wife."

"In a moment. It has to be tonight, is that clear?"

"Hold on." I put my hand over the receiver. "It's Boggs," I told Padillo. "They'll go along with Dymec, but they want to see him tonight. It's tonight or never, according to him."

"Set it up for Seventh Street at midnight. I can get Dymec."

"It can be arranged for midnight," I said into the phone. I gave him the Seventh Street address.

"Tell him he'd better start getting the money together," Padillo said.

"Don't forget the money," I said. "If he's not sure of the money, he'll walk out."

"That's being taken care of," Boggs said. "But the money's to go to Padillo, right?"

"Right."

"He'll have it tomorrow."

"Put my wife on."

"I'll see you at midnight, McCorkle. Here's your wife."

"Fredl?"

"I'm on, darling. I'm doing fine; it's just a little tiring and I miss you so much."

"It'll be over soon; it's near the end now."

"It seems so long. It seems longer than forever. hope—"

The telephone went dead and I placed it in its cradle and signaled a waiter to take it away, but Padillo told him to leave it for a moment.

"She all right?" Padillo asked.

"I guess so; I couldn't tell. She didn't scream anyway."

"Has she screamed before?" Sylvia asked.

"Once. They made her scream to impress me. They succeeded."

"They're rotten!" she said and I was surprised by the intensity in her voice. "They kill and they hurt and they don't leave you anything. Then they laugh about it. I've heard them laugh when someone was hurt. Their big, loud laughs."

"Maybe they laugh because they're afraid," Padillo said quietly. "I've seen frightened people laugh."

"Are you apologizing for them?" she demanded.

"I don't apologize for anyone," he said. "I have trouble enough finding excuses for myself."

He picked up the phone and dialed a number. It seemed to take a long time for it to answer. "This is Padillo. You have an appointment at midnight on Seventh Street with your future employers. McCorkle will be there. I can't make it." He listened for a while. "Just you and McCorkle. I'll talk to you tomorrow."

He replaced the phone and the waiter took it away and plugged it in at another table where some customer probably wanted to call Honolulu. If he did, we added twenty per cent. The food came and it looked good, but I wasn't hungry. Herr Horst went by and stopped to find out whether something was wrong and I assured him that it wasn't.

"You can miss a meal," Padillo said. "In fact, you could miss two or three."

"You think I've filled out a bit?"

"It gives you dignity. You're losing that lean, raffish look."

"Care for some coffee?" I asked Sylvia.

"Please."

"You try," I told Padillo. "I want to see how well Horst has passed the word to the staff."

Padillo looked up, nodded his head slightly, and a waiter was hovering at his elbow. It could have been Herr Horst's instructions about the new active partner, or it could have been Padillo. I had seen him command attention like that in restaurants where he dined for the first time. If it were a trick, it was one I wanted to learn.

He ordered the coffee and none of us wanted dessert.

"When your meeting with Boggs and Dymec is over," Padillo said, "it might be a good idea to let Boggs leave first. Then stall Dymec for ten minutes or so. I don't want them to have the chance to do any negotiating on the side."

"Don't you trust anyone?" Sylvia asked.

"I'm careful."

"It must get lonely."

"There's usually someone around with big cinnamon eyes who seems to think so—and wants to do something about it."

"It could be a challenge, but one I could easily resist," she said.

"Then I'll keep on being lonely for a while."

Sylvia turned to me. "Your business associate doesn't go out of his way to be friendly, does he?"

"I'm surprised," I said. "I've never seen that line fail before. It's been used often enough."

"I'm out of practice," Padillo said. He looked at his watch. "It's eleven o'clock Saturday night and I understand the town has an hour to go before the curfew of the Sabbath. How would you like to go pub-crawling?"

"With you?" she said.

"I'm as harmless as McCorkle."

"I'm not dead, just married," I reminded him.

"I think you're fine," she said.

"We'll call it a comparison shopping tour to see if anyone has better graffiti than ours." This time he smiled.

Sylvia turned to me. "Is it all right?"

"If he gets his glass of warm milk at one, he'll be fine," I said.

Padillo rose and helped the girl with her chair. I took a key off my ring and handed it to her. "This is a spare to my apartment."

"Call me when you get back," Padillo said.

"I will."

"Where should we go?" Padillo asked.

"Try M Street in Georgetown," I said. "There's a whole string of bars there, or at least they were there last week. They have some very cute names—new ones every other day or so."

I watched them leave, the slender young girl with the helmet of blonde hair and an up-from-under look that could melt a hangman's heart, and the partner, not that young nor nearly so, with the tanned, quiet, hard face and the effortless movement that's seldom seen in a human and always in a cat.

They were, as the town's frosty-eyed society writers would have it, a striking couple, and the customers forgot about their steaks long enough to look at them as they went by. They didn't seem to notice the two FBI men who followed along behind. I ordered more coffee and a brandy and after being served, I watched the customers for a while. There didn't seem to be any poor ones. Most were too round in the belly or too sparse on top. Their laughter was too loud and too long and too hard. But then I'd seldom heard happy laughter in a saloon, and I had been listening for a long time.

I didn't like my customers that night and I wasn't too wild about myself. I wondered what Fredl was doing and where she was and what she was thinking. I wondered where the customers would go when they stopped eating and drinking at midnight. I wondered if they had homes, or if they ever quit talking and chewing and swallowing because I never saw them unless their jaws were moving.

It was eleven-thirty by the time I decided to catch a cab and go down to Seventh Street and talk to a couple of men who wanted to kill a Prime Minister. It seemed as good a way as any to wind up Saturday night in the capital of the world.

By no means a new hand at intrigue, I had the cab driver let me out two blocks away from the dingy office. It was ten minutes to twelve and Seventh Street was almost dead except for a couple of drunks moving slowly and carefully down the opposite sidewalk. I let myself into the office, turned on the light, and pulled down the cracked green shade. The dust was still on the blotter. I sat behind the desk to wait. Boggs was the first to arrive. He looked around the office and didn't seem to like what he saw. I didn't feel up to an apology.

"You reached your man?" he asked.

"We reached him."

"He's not here."

"If he were here, he'd be three minutes early."

He grunted something at that and brushed off one of the folding metal chairs and sat down. I propped my feet on the desk, smoked a cigarette, and carefully dropped the ashes on the floor.

"Your man knows what he's supposed to do?"

"He knows."

"What should I tell him?"

"Tell him everything—the where and the when to begin with. He'll have to check it all out. If you have a how let him in on that, too. He has the who and the money is the why. You needn't go into your lecture on the humanitarian service he's performing. He wouldn't understand what you're talking about."

"You have a low opinion of us, don't you, McCorkle? And it's not just because of your wife."

"I think you're aces," I said, and blew some smoke rings at the ceiling.

Dymec came in and gave us his grave nod. He took a seat. It was the same one he had sat in that morning.

"All right," I said, swinging my feet off the desk. "I'm the interlocutor. This is Jon and this is Wendell. I don't think we need any more names than that. Jon knows what he's supposed to do. You can give him the details."

"Shall we talk about money first?" Dymec asked.

"You talk about money with Padillo," I said.

Dymec nodded. "Very well."

"I have a map here of Washington," Boggs said. "Are you familiar with the city?" He spread the map on the desk.

"With the northwest section and Capitol Hill," Dymec said.

"Good. On Tuesday we are to be given an official tour.

We start at the State Department, go up to the Washington Monument, then to the Jefferson Memorial, then to the Capitol, down Independence past the Rayburn Building, and we turn left on Seventh Street—this street, isn't it? but farther up—and down to Constitution Avenue. We continue up Constitution Avenue and follow it to Seventeenth where we turn north toward Pennsylvania Avenue. At Eighteenth and Pennsylvania—just across the street from the USIA—we turn up north on Eighteenth and proceed to Connecticut Avenue and Dupont Circle." He paused and looked at Dymec.

"We must never make that turn up Eighteenth."

Dymec nodded. "It's to take place here then," and he jabbed a forefinger at the block between Seventeenth and Eighteenth on Pennsylvania.

"Yes."

"What time of day will it be?"

"The tour starts at two from the State Department. We should be here between two-forty-five and three."

"How many cars will there be in the tour?"

"Four."

"Your man will be in an open car?"

"We have specified that."

"If it rains?"

"We have the long-range forecast. It says that it won't."

"If it does?" Dymec asked again.

Boggs shrugged. "It's off."

"How much security will there be?"

"The minimum."

"How much is that? Do you know?"

"There will be four motorcycle riders. Two in front; two in the rear."

"Have there been any threats on his life? Anything that would cause them to add security personnel?"

"None that they have revealed to us. Your countrymen, McCorkle, are seemingly indifferent to what happens in Africa."

"Most of them don't care about what happens here, as long as it happens in the next block."

"This building on the northeast corner of Eighteenth and Pennsylvania. It's the Roger Smith Hotel," Dymec said.

"Right."

"Why choose it?"

"Because of the roof garden. It's deserted this time of year. You won't need to reserve a room."

"I'll have to take a look at it."

"Of course."

"Where will your man be seated?" Dymec asked.

"There will be three in the back. He will be in the center."

"Who will be driving?"

"My colleague."

"He will go slowly?"

"He'll probably go around the block if you miss the first time," I said.

Boggs didn't find that amusing; neither did Dymec. He was all business.

Boggs had another question: "What kind of weapon do you plan to use?"

"I haven't decided."

"My Prime Minister has expressed a preference."

"What is it?"

"He prefers not to be shot with a gun of English manufacture."

— SIXTEEN —

When Boggs was at the door he turned to me and said: "I'll be in touch with you tomorrow."

"All right."

"You'll continue with the planning?"

"Yes."

"There must be no mistakes."

"We can't control the weather."

He nodded slightly. "True. But if you're a religious man, you should pray. If not, you should hope very hard."

"I'll see what I can do."

He looked at Dymec and the Pole stared back at him with his expressionless slate-colored eyes.

"We may not meet again."

Dymec just nodded; he said nothing.

"Your reputation is encouraging. I advise you to do nothing to diminish it."

"I know my job," Dymec said. "If the other arrangements are properly made, my performance will be satisfactory."

Boggs looked as if he wanted to say something else, but changed his mind, and opened the door. "Good night," he said and left.

I waited until I could no longer hear his footsteps on the stairs.

"What kind of rifle do you want?" I asked.

Dymec shrugged. "Since I won't be using it, anything will do."

"Suppose you were going to use it, what would you want?"

"A Winchester Model 70, the target rifle with a 4x scope and two rounds of .30-06."

"You need two rounds?"

"No. I only need one. But there's always the chance of a misfire."

"We'll try to find it, but you may have to settle for something less sporting."

Dymec yawned and stretched. He seemed bored by the whole thing. "How far will this farce be carried?"

"As far as necessary."

"Have you learned where they're holding your wife?"

"No."

"It would seem to me that your entire scheme depends on that. If you don't find her, you may wish me to carry out the actual assignment. I'll be glad to, of course, but it will cost you a little more."

"We hope to avoid that."

He yawned again. He was either bored or it was far past his bedtime. "Of course. But if you do change your mind, I'll cooperate—for a slight additional fee."

"To satisfy an idle curiosity, just what do you consider a slight additional fee?"

"In the neighborhood of ten thousand dollars."

"That's a high-class neighborhood."

"There would be no shares to the other two, either."

"I'll keep it in mind," I told him. "When do you plan to look the hotel over?"

"Tomorrow. Early tomorrow morning I think would be best. It should be quiet then."

"We'll meet with Padillo tomorrow."

"He knows how to reach me."

He stood up and moved towards the door. "Your friend from Africa seemed a bit edgy."

"I suppose he doesn't do this every day."

"Probably not." He yawned once more, but this time he remembered to cover it with his hand. "Well, good night."

"Good night," I said. "Pleasant dreams."

Dymec left and I listened to his footsteps clatter down the stairs. I got up and walked over to the window and peeked out around the edge of the shade. A dark blue or black car was parked across the street and down some seventy-five feet. It turned on its lights as Dymec came out of the building. He looked up at the window, then hurried across the street and got into the car. It started up and sped by the window. I didn't get the license number. There was really no need. Boggs was the driver. I assumed Dymec was no longer yawning.

I crossed over to the desk and dialed Padillo's number. There was no answer. I turned off the lights, made sure the door was locked, and walked down the stairs. I looked for a cab, but there was none. A man shuffled out of the shadows and touched me on the arm.

"Friend, I won't lie to you," he said. "I need a drink bad."

"So do I," I said, and gave him fifty cents and he God-blessed me and moved on down the street. There seemed to be a little more spring to his step. I wondered where he bought his drinks after the bars were closed. A cab came by and the driver looked me over carefully before he stopped.

"Can't be too careful down here," he said. "You can get all sorts of loonies."

He chattered away some more about the hardships of a cab driver's life, but I didn't listen. I was brooding about my own troubles. He let me out at my apartment building and I pretended not to notice the car with the two men that was parked across the street.

I got off the elevator and opened my door. Padillo and Sylvia Underhill were sitting on the couch. She looked a little flustered, but Padillo seemed calm enough as he wiped away the lipstick.

"I'll knock next time," I said and crossed over to the bar. When I had the drink I moved over to my favorite chair and sat down. "You kiddies have a good evening? Your chaperones are across the street."

"The teeny-boppers on M Street seemed to enjoy themselves," Padillo said. "How do we avoid them?"

"I keep raising the prices," I said. "They think they're being exploited."

"How'd your session go?" he asked.

"Fine. Just fine," I said. "Dymec's crossing us. Boggs left first. Dymec stayed for five or ten minutes. When he left I peeked and saw him get into Boggs's car."

Padillo nodded. "I thought he would. The other question is whether Magda or Price will cross with him."

"You expected him to go over?"

"Five minutes after I made him the proposition, he was on the phone."

"With whom?"

"With whoever's running him for the Poles and then with the Africans."

"I thought you'd doubled him."

Padillo smiled. "I did. But this is too good. He can't pass it up. They'll tell him to go ahead and get rid of the old man. The propaganda value to them is as much or more than it would be to Boggs and Darragh. He wouldn't tell his President about me. He can't or he'd expose his moonlighting for the U.S. He probably said that he was indirectly approached and wanted instructions. The information alone will keep them smiling in Warsaw for days. If it comes off, they'll be even happier."

"Sometimes," I said, "not every day, of course, but sometimes you might just give me an idea of what you're up to."

"I did," he said. "I told you to keep Dymec there for ten minutes or so after Boggs left. If you'd let them leave together, they'd have thought you were setting them up. This way it's their own idea."

"What if I hadn't looked out the window?"

"I'd have been disappointed in you."

"But it wouldn't have mattered?"

"Not really. Of the three of them, I figured Dymec for the cross although Magda is also a likely candidate. He'll probably swing her over to make sure we don't get to Fredl."

I put my drink down carefully on a coaster and lighted a cigarette. "So of the three people you brought in, two of them are going to cross us."

"I told you we couldn't do it alone. If I couldn't have counted on at least one of them crossing, I wouldn't have brought them in."

"Perhaps you'd better tell him?" Sylvia said to Padillo.

He turned and smiled at her. "You think so?"

"Don't bother," I said. "It's pleasant here in the dark."

"They have a saying in my country," she said. "When the lion is coming at you, you make a plan. We made one tonight."

"I made it," Padillo said. "Like most of my plans, it involves someone else's neck being risked."

"Whose?"

"Sylvia's."

"For what purpose?"

"So we can find out where they're keeping Fredl."

"It's a wonderful plan," Sylvia said. Her face seemed to glow with excitement. With most of her lipstick on Padillo's collar, she looked younger than twenty-one. She looked about fifteen.

"You conned her," I said to him.

He nodded. "That's right."

"What does she have to do that might get her killed?" I turned to the girl. "Don't let him kid you with that casual understated manner of his. If he says there might be a slight danger, you can bet on the roof falling in. If he says you'll risk your neck, it means that you'll actually have to stick it into the noose, let them spring the trap, and hope somebody will catch you before you drop. He doesn't have any safe plans. He thinks everyone carries the same rabbit's foot he does."

"I know," she said softly. "But it's a good plan."

"It's not that good," Padillo said. "It's just the only one we've got."

"And it puts us on to Fredl?"

"It should."

"All right," I said. "Let's hear it."

"Sylvia goes to the trade mission and tells them that she knows all about the deal to kill Van Zandt."

"And then they kill her. That's not bad."

"They won't kill her."

"They killed her father."

"I'm not saying they're not hard enough to kill her; they're just not smart enough."

"What if one of them has an inspiration?"

"That's the chance she'll take."

"Right through the noose, kid. Just like I told you."

"I know them," she said. "I know what they are. But they won't kill me while Van Zandt's around."

"He didn't seem too particular about my wife."

"But they wouldn't do it at the trade mission," she said. "They don't butcher their pigs in their homes."

"So they take you someplace else," I said. "They take you to where they're holding Fredl."

"That's it," Padillo said.

"And we follow along in the Stingray with the top down."

"Hardman."

I ran a hand through my hair and felt how thin it was getting, but who wants fat hair? "I haven't got anything better. When does it all happen?"

"Tuesday morning," Padillo said.

"Hardman can't do it alone."

"No."

"Who'll be with him—Mush?"

"We'll need Mush."

"I want to meet whoever's with Hardman."

"So do I," Padillo said.

"How many do you think he'll need?"

"Three."

"He can get them, but this is going to cost."

"It's my tab," Padillo said. "If that's important."

"It isn't. Why Tuesday morning?"

"One, because they won't have time to kill Sylvia. They'll have to get rid of her and they'll probably take her straight over to where Fredl's being held and leave her. Two, because you'll have to figure out some way to tip Fredl off the next time you talk to her."

"I'll think of something."

Padillo got up and crossed over to the bar. "Scotch?"

"Fine."

"Sylvia?"

"Nothing, thank you. Could I make some coffee?"

"It's instant."

"It was fine this afternoon."

She went into the kitchen and ran some water into the kettle. Padillo crossed the room and handed me my drink.

"Can you think of anything better?" he asked in a low voice.

I shook my head no. "How much charm did you have to turn on?"

"She's a nice kid. I don't want anything to happen to her. Or to Fredl."

"But there's a damned good chance."

"Yes."

"What did you have in mind if she hadn't turned up?"

He smiled, but there was nothing bright or warm in it. "Magda," he said.

"The same thing?"

"Very similar, but with one difference."

"What?"

"Magda would get killed."

"I don't think I need the details."

"I didn't think you would."

Sylvia came in with her cup of coffee. She sat beside Padillo on the couch.

"If either of you think that you're using me, I want you to forget it," she said. "I've known these people all my life and I suppose I was brought up to hold them in contempt, but never to underestimate their viciousness. I've seen them do horrible things to people in my country— really shocking, awful things, and I've heard descriptions of worse." She turned to Padillo and her eyes looked directly into his. "I may be naive about many things, about you in particular, but I am not naive about them. I know them and I know the risk I'm taking. I was sent here by people who are the last chance that my country has, to do what I could. This seems to be the best I can do and I plan to do it."

"All right," Padillo said. "We'll go ahead. The first thing is to get in touch with Hardman. Where do you think he'd be?"

"God knows," I said. "Let me try that Cadillac of his." I picked up the phone and called the mobile operator and gave her the number. There were a few beeps and buzzes and then his voice came on.

"Hard-man here," he said.

"This is McCorkle."

"How you, baby?"

"Fine."

"What you heard bout Fredl?"

"That's why I called. Where are you?"

"Cruisin around on upper Fourteenth. You home?"

"Yes."

"Want me to come over?"

"I think it would be a good idea."

"Be there in fifteen, twenty minutes."

"You alone?"

"Betty's with me. Be okay? She'll keep her mouth shut."

"Okay."

I hung up and turned to Padillo and Sylvia. "He'll be here in fifteen or twenty minutes. He's bringing Betty."

Padillo nodded. "She probably knows all about it by now anyway."

"Is there anybody in town who doesn't?" I asked.

— SEVENTEEN —

Hardman was wearing a double-breasted camel's hair coat and alligator shoes. When he took off the coat you could admire his dark green cashmere jacket, his fawn-colored slacks, and the yellow ascot that he wore at the throat of a pale green velour shirt. He was everything the well-dressed numbers man should be and I asked him how Trueblue Sue had done in the fourth at Shenandoah.

"Out of the money, baby, I'm sorry to say."

I introduced Hardman and Betty to Sylvia Underhill. I took Betty's mink and hung it up carefully, the way five thousand dollars should be hung up. Padillo mixed them a drink and they sat in two easy chairs. Betty was wearing some kind of black-and-white-striped bellbottomed lounging pajamas that either were going to be the rage that year, or the year after.

"What you got going?" Hardman said.

"We think we've got a plan to find Fredl," I said, "but we're going to need some help."

"Keep talkin."

I let Padillo tell it. He told it quickly and concisely. Hardman didn't interrupt or say anything until Padillo stopped talking.

"Four could probably do it," Hardman said. "Me and three others. We pick em up out on Mass Avenue and then trade off on the tail job. We can use phones to stay in touch. But you ain't got no idea where she's gonna go?"

"None."

"Need a moving van then."

"Why?" I said.

"You get four colored boys pulling up before some house in a white neighborhood and getting out of two cars and moving up to that house and you got law. Especially if you have to rush out of there with two white girls. But with a moving van, us dressed in white coveralls, and maybe a pick-up truck for the wheel man—one of those fancy jobs that don't carry much and are built like a sedan almost, it could work okay."

"Can you get the three you need?" Padillo said.

Hardman looked down at the toe of his right shoe and polished it against the back of his left leg. "This ain't gonna be no cheapie."

"We'll take care of the money," I said.

"Might run you high—ten, fifteen thousand. That includes any—well, any accidents that might happen."

"Make it fifteen thousand and if it costs any more we'll take care of it," Padillo said.

Hardman looked at Betty. "What you think, honey?"

"You use Mush, Tulip and Nineball, it cost you that."

"I was thinking of them."

"We need Mush for something else," Padillo said.

"We get Johnny Jay then," Hardman said.

"We want to stay in touch with you from the time you pick Sylvia up until the time you're done," Padillo said. "Will phones work?"

"We set up a conference call and keep it goin till we're done."

"Operators listen in?" I asked.

"Ain't the operators you have to worry about. Those mobile phones are seventy-five-man party lines. You get an hour's worth of calls a month for six dollars. After that it's about thirty cents for ten minutes and after that ten cents a minute."

"Can you make a conference call?" Padillo said.

"Sure."

"And keep it going for as long as you want?"

"You payin for it; you can talk for hours."

"Then what we say can't make any sense."

"That shouldn't be hard."

"What about getting the phones installed?"

Hardman sighed. "I already got one in mine, so you can use my car. Mush got one in his. That takes care of two. We gonna have to get two more—one in the truck and one in the pickup. That'll cost us a little. Have to get a man to juggle some orders at the telephone company, but I know the man to get hold of." He paused and looked at his shoes again. "Have to get the trucks and get them painted, think up a name for the moving company, call it Acme or something like that. How about Four-Square?"

"Fine," I said.

"How many you think's gonna be in this place we gotta get Fredl and Missy here out of?" Hardman said.

"Two, maybe three," Padillo said.

"They gonna put up a fuss?"

"You can count on it."

"After we find out where it's at, how soon we go in?"

"As soon as whoever brings her there leaves," Padillo said.

"Where you want us to take em, once we get em out?"

"My place, Hard," Betty said. "I get Doctor Lambert down to look at his wife."

"You wanta meet these boys who gonna work with me?"

"What do you think?" Padillo asked.

"They might be wanting a little advance."

"All right. Let's meet tomorrow afternoon on Seventh Street. That okay?"

"Two o'clock Sunday?" Hardman said.

"Fine."

"One thing," I said to Hardman, "no hot cars."

"You ain't making it no easier."

"No cops," I said.

"I couldn't see too good, but looks like a couple of them are camped outside right now," Hardman said. "They for you or somebody else?"

"They just want to make sure Padillo gets home all right."

"They don't look like metros."

"They aren't; they're FBI," I said.

"They ain't in on this, is they?"

"No. They'll be out of the picture by Monday."

"I sure don't want no Federals," Hardman said. "They nothing but bad times."

"They'll be out," I said.

He turned to Sylvia. "Missy, you bein awful quiet over there."

She smiled. "It's going so fast. I suppose I'm really not used to it."

"You be all right," he said. "The Hard-man'll take care of you."

"There's one other thing, Hardman," Padillo said.

"What's that?"

"Sylvia is going to drive out to the trade mission on Massachusetts, get out of her car, and go in. If they don't bring her out in thirty minutes, I want you to go in and get her."

"Uh-huh," Hardman said. "Now that's where the power is?"

"That's right."

"That's where all those African ofays are?"

"Yes."

"Price have to go up on that." He held up a big hand. "Not me now. I go in after her and all. But the other three might get a little dicey unless there's a bonus."

"There'll be one, if you have to go in."

"They got a back way out of that place—alley entrance maybe?"

"I don't know," I said. "You'd better check it out."

"I'll do that tomorrow," he said.

"Like another drink?" I asked.

He looked at his watch. "It's two-thirty now. I gotta start roundin up these folks. We best be goin." They rose and I got up and brought them their coats.

"Nice meetin you, Missy," Hardman said to Sylvia.

"Thank you."

"Don't worry about nothin."

"I'll try not to."

Hardman and Betty were at the door when the big man turned. "What you gonna use Mush for, baby?" he asked Padillo.

"I'm not sure yet."

169

"He wants to learn that sidestep thing you did on him real bad."

"I'll teach it to him."

"How those three friends of yours workin out?"

"About like I expected."

"Mush gonna be round them?"

"Probably."

"He be a good man for that."

"That's what I thought," Padillo said.

Hardman turned to me. "We'll get Fredl out okay, Mac."

"I believe it."

"See you Sunday about two. Hell, it's already Sunday." They left quickly.

I walked over to the bar and poured a drink for myself. "Care for a nightcap?"

"If that's a hint, I'll take it," Padillo said. I poured him one.

"Sylvia?"

"No thank you."

I handed Padillo his drink and said: "You cut it a little thin, didn't you?"

"On the half-hour thing?"

"Yes."

"I don't think so. They'll move fast, once Sylvia gets in. They should have her out within fifteen minutes. If it's more than a half-hour, then they'll be thinking of doing something else."

"I was just thinking about your two friends waiting patiently in that car downstairs," I said. "If Hardman had been sent by your mythical Portuguese, he could have taken the elevator up, done you in leisurely, had a couple of drinks, and then gone home to bed. If they're protection, they don't add up to much."

"Did you get a good look at them?" he asked.

"No."

"They won't be the same ones who were at the bar earlier. We lost them in Georgetown."

"We went out a back door," Sylvia said.

"Who are they?"

"I'd like to make sure." He finished his drink and stood up. "You care to join me?"

"Not really, but I will."

"We'll be back shortly," he told Sylvia as I opened the door.

We walked down the hall to the elevator and I punched the button.

"They're not FBIs?" I said.

He shook his head. "I lost them at the fourth bar we hit. We weren't followed here. I doubt that they'd sit outside waiting for me. They'd have made sure I was in your place. They're supposed to be protecting me, not just pulling a surveillance job. I'd say the FBI pair, or their relief, is waiting for me in the lobby of the Mayflower."

"Who's out front?"

The elevator came and we got in. Padillo took his revolver out of his topcoat pocket and tucked it into the waistband of his trousers.

"Let's find out."

The elevator stopped at the lobby and we got out and walked to the thick glass entrance doors. I could see the car across the street, about thirty feet to the left. The two men were still in it, their faces turned towards us, but obscured by their hats. They saw us coming through the

apartment doors and the one nearest the street and neares
to us rolled down his window.

"When we get to the end of the sidewalk," Padillo said
"shake hands with me, turn around, and go back to th
lobby. I'll go the left. Walk to the lobby and turn around.

We got to the end of the sidewalk and we shook hands
"I'll see you tomorrow," Padillo said, more loudly than h
normally would, and started walking slowly to his left.
moved quickly to the door of the lobby and turned. I coul
see Padillo as he drew parallel with the car across th
street. The car's engine started. Padillo dived for the law
to his left and while he was in the air somebody shot a
him. He rolled as he hit the ground and came up with th
revolver in his hand. The man in the righthand seat of th
car fired again, but the car was moving. The shot echoe
as the sound waves bounced between the apartment build
ings. The car was a grey Ford Galaxie and its tires squeale
for what seemed to be seconds as they spun away from
the curb. I watched its taillights blink when the driver hi
the brake to make the corner. The car skidded as it turne
and then it was gone. Some lights came on in an apartmen
across the street. Padillo ran back to the lobby doors an
we moved quickly to the elevator. It was still at the groun
level and we got inside and I punched the button for m
floor. Padillo was holding his left side and biting his lowe
lip.

"Hurt?" I asked.

"Like hell," he said.

"You moved really pretty. What tipped you off?"

"You get a good look at them?"

"No."

"I did when I was right across the street from them."

"Recognize anyone?"

"Not the one at the wheel. Just the passenger." The elevator stopped at my floor and we got out and walked quickly down the hall. I put the key in the lock and turned it.

"Who was it?"

"Our British cousin," he said. "Philip Price."

— EIGHTEEN —

I was watching Sylvia Underhill tape a new bandage to
Padillo's side when the phone rang. I answered it and
a male voice asked for Mr. Michael Padillo. I passed him
the phone and he talked briefly, mostly in monosyllables,
and then hung up.

"That was one of our friends from the FBI," he said.
"They're getting tired of sitting around the lobby of the
hotel, so they called Iker. He suggested that they call here.
I told them to go home."

"How does that feel?" Sylvia asked.

Padillo looked down at the bandage. It was a neat job.
"Much better, thank you."

He picked up his shirt and started putting it on. He only
winced slightly when he poked his left arm through the
sleeve.

"You may as well stay here tonight," I said. "If Price
is looking for you—" I let the sentence trail off.

"He won't be looking any more tonight."

"Do you think he knows that you saw him?"

"I doubt it. He was counting on surprise and didn't know I was curious about who was in the car. He'll show tomorrow when we split the money—if we get it from Boggs."

"He said he'd have it."

"I'll call the trio tomorrow and set the meeting for eleven at Seventh Street," Padillo said. "Price will be there, tweedy as hell, and looking as if he's just come from communion."

"Only one more thing," I said.

"Why did he take a shot at me?" Padillo said.

"That occurred to me."

"Somebody must have told him to."

"Who?"

"I could give you a list."

"You have no idea?"

Padillo shook his head. "None."

I stood up and looked at my watch. "It's now three-thirty of a Sunday morning. There are extra toothbrushes in the medicine cabinet. You can argue about who gets the couch if you want to, or work out your own sleeping arrangements. I'm no gentleman. I'm using my own bed."

"We'll figure something out," Padillo said. Sylvia suddenly became busy putting adhesive tape and the gauze back in the first aid kit.

I walked over to the bar and poured myself a drink. "I'll say good night. The alarm will be set for eight. With luck, I won't hear it."

I went into the bedroom, stripped off my clothes, and sat on the edge of the bed and smoked a cigarette and sipped the Scotch. I set the alarm and put out the cigarette. It had been a long, hard day. I lay back on the bed and closed my eyes. When I opened them again the alarm was ringing and I realized I had to get up and start all over again.

It hardly seemed worthwhile.

I stood in the shower for ten minutes and let the hot water beat on my neck. Then I turned it off. I didn't try the cold although they say it opens your pores. I didn't care whether mine were open or closed. Shaving was a problem, but I got through it without cutting anything important, and after I brushed my teeth, I congratulated myself again on the fact that they were all mine. There were a couple of nice gold crowns, far back, but essentially they were the original equipment. I combed my hair, which seemed to take less and less time each day, and then there was nothing else to do but get dressed and meet the new day which would probably be worse than yesterday but better than tomorrow.

Padillo was dressed and sitting on the couch holding a cup of coffee and a cigarette when I crossed the livingroom towards the kitchen.

"The water's hot," he said.

"Uh."

I poured some on top of the coffee, put in a spoonful of sugar, and stirred. I picked up the cup and saucer and went back into the livingroom and sat down carefully. I tried the coffee.

"They've got it foolproof," I said. "It's impossible to make a good cup."

"Uh."

"She still asleep?"

"I think so."

"How's your side?"

"Stiff."

"How was the couch?"

"I wouldn't know."

I didn't have any more questions. Padillo got up and walked into the kitchen and made himself another cup of coffee. The door chimes rang as he came back into the livingroom. I got up and answered the door. It was the thin man who had let us into the trade mission, still wearing his black suit and his grave manner.

"Mr. Boggs asked that I deliver this," he said and handed me a brown paper sack, the kind that you bring the week's groceries home in. I took it, unfolded the top, and looked inside. There was a lot of money inside.

"Do you want me to sign anything?" I said.

The thin man permitted himself a smile. "That won't be necessary. Mr. Boggs said he himself would deliver the remainder."

"Thank Mr. Boggs for me."

"Yes, sir," the thin man said and turned to leave. I closed the door.

"What is it?" Padillo asked.

"Money. A whole lot of money."

I walked over to the couch and handed him the sack. "They didn't have time to get it wrapped."

He took the sack and dumped the money on the coffee table. It was in fifty- and one-hundred-dollar bills and it seemed to give off a nice glow.

"You want to count it?" Padillo said.

"It's a little early for me; I doubt if I could get past nineteen."

Padillo leaned back on the couch and closed his eyes tightly. His left hand moved to his side. "Ouch," he said.

"You didn't put much feeling into that."

"There should be $37,500 there."

"All right. I'll count it."

The fifties were in packets of one thousand dollars. There were fifteen of them. The hundreds were wrapped up in two-thousand-dollar packets, eleven in all. There was some loose change consisting of two one-hundred-dollar bills and six fifties that made up the remaining five hundred.

"It's all here," I said. "You want me to divide it into three tidy piles?"

Padillo sat up and his face was pale beneath his deep tan. "Half in one pile, split the remainder. It's a two-one-one cut remember."

I did some mental arithmetic. "The bills are the wrong size. A fourth would be $9,375."

"Do the best you can," Padillo said, his eyes still closed.

I went back into the kitchen for another cup of coffee while Padillo pulled the telephone over and started dialing. He had only to speak a few words to complete each call. By the time I got back into the livingroom he was finishing his last one. He put the phone away.

"That was Price," he said.

"How'd he sound?"

"Sleepy, but greedy."

"And the other two?"

"They'll be there at eleven."

I indicated the money on the table. "What shall we do with it?"

"Have you got a briefcase?"

"I'll get it." I went into the bedroom and pulled an attaché case out of the closet. Someone had given it to me years ago and for a while I had tried to think of some way of using it, but had finally given up and just put it away. It was a black leather case with solid silver fittings. If I'd been in some other line of work, I could have carried my lunch in it. I handed the case to Padillo.

"You have any rubberbands?"

"Fredl saves them. She puts them on the kitchen door-knob." I got three off the knob, gave them to Padillo, and he snapped them around the stacks of money and put the bills into the briefcase and closed it.

"I lost the key," I said.

"It doesn't matter."

The door chimes rang again and I looked at Padillo. "It's your house," he said.

"But it's your popularity."

I crossed the room and opened the door. The man who stood there wore a plaid sports jacket, an open blue flannel shirt, dark gray slacks and three vertical creases in his forehead. It was a sign he was thinking. His name was Stan Burmser and he had once been able to tell Padillo where he should go in Europe and what he should do when he got there. I hadn't seen him in more than a year. It had been in Bonn and even then he had been wearing the three vertical creases in his forehead. He seemed to think a lot.

"Hello, Burmser," I said.

He smiled and the creases disappeared. The smile was as friendly as a fifth letter from the finance company. "I'm looking for Padillo."

"Your search is ended." I stepped back and held the door open. "A Mr. Burmser to see you."

Padillo didn't get up nor did he say anything. He watched Burmser cross the room and stand in front of him. Burmser had his hands stuck deep in his jacket pockets. He rocked back and forth on his heels as he stared at Padillo for what seemed to be long moments.

"We got a report two days ago that you were back," Burmser said.

Padillo nodded. "Still got your trade-off with the FBI. The one-way trade."

"They make mistakes sometimes."

"And you just dropped by at nine o'clock in the morning to make sure. You'll be late for Sunday School."

"I'm Catholic."

"Funny, you don't look it."

"You still have those tired old jokes."

"One gets fond of them."

"I've got a new one. It was too good to keep. That's why I came over myself."

"I'm ready."

"You're marked, Padillo. You're in the book."

"That's not new. I've been in somebody or other's book for years."

"Not in this one. The British have got you down and they've got it assigned."

"They wouldn't tell you about it if they did."

"You're not the only one who's doubled a few."

"I suppose not."

"And that's what's so funny."

"I bet you're coming to the punch-line now."

Burmser's grin got wider. "That's right. I am. They handed the assignment to someone you yourself doubled. They handed it to Philip Price."

"What have they got against me?" Padillo asked. He could have been asking if the bus stopped here, or across the street.

"I don't know; I don't really care."

"Then why travel all the way in from McLean to tell me about it?"

"I live in Cleveland Park."

"It must be pretty there in the fall."

"Price is good. You doubled him; you should know how good he is."

"He also works for you."

"That's right, he does."

"You could call him off."

"I could, but the British would have too many questions for him if he didn't carry out his assignment. It might bust him wide open. He's been fairly useful to us. We'd like him to continue that way."

"And I'm not," Padillo said.

Burmser quit smiling. "You're nothing to us, Padillo. We've wiped you off. There isn't a trace of you left. You never existed as far as we're concerned."

"How far back did you go?"

"All the way."

Padillo smiled. "That's a lot of territory and a lot of years. Why tell me about it?"

"I was told to."

"I must have a friend left some place in the organization."

"One is all."

Padillo shrugged. "All right, Burmser, you got to play Old Blind Pew and pass out the black spot this morning. Anything else?"

"Just this: We never heard of you. If you're in trouble, you're alone. There won't be any phone calls, no hush-ups. The fix won't be put in anywhere. You've wanted out for a long time, Padillo, and now you are. As far as we're concerned you're a Mexican or a Spaniard who's in this country illegally, but we're not even sure about that, because we never heard of you. You're nothing." Burmser was breathing a little hard when he was through.

Padillo turned to me: "You think I should tell the shop steward about this?"

"Ask him about what happens to all the money you've contributed to the pension plan."

Burmser smiled his final-notice smile. "You're breaking me up. But, gentlemen, I've enjoyed it." He turned and headed for the door. When he was there he stopped with his hand on the knob. "You were pretty good at one time, Padillo. Pretty good or lucky. Now you'd better be both."

"Tell the old gang hello for me," Padillo said.

Burmser looked at Padillo. "They never heard of you," he said. He opened the door and left.

"He enjoyed himself," I said.

"But he cleared Price up."

"I'd say that Price told the British that you were actually going to shoot Van Zandt and they told him to take you out."

"So it seems."

"What's Price after, a pat on the head?"

"A bonus."

"From whom?"

"The British. He tells them that I'm planning the attempt, they tell him to take me out, and he does. They'll give him a bonus."

"What then?"

"He hooks up with Dymec to do the assassination for real."

"Now you can tell me that this is all in keeping with the master plan. The one you have written down on the back of a match book."

"More or less." He walked into the kitchen with the

cup and saucer. When he came back, I asked him: "What's the less part?"

"I hadn't planned on making a hero out of Price. But now we're going to have to."

— NINETEEN —

Sylvia Underhill walked in from the bedroom before Padillo could tell me the rest of the master plan—or make it up—I was never sure which. He stopped talking and we both said good morning.

"I heard you with someone and I thought I'd overslept," she said. She was wearing a blue wool suit with big white buttons and the warm glow on her face seemed a little radiant to be the result of just six hours' sleep.

"An old acquaintance dropped by," Padillo said. "He couldn't stay long."

"May I cook breakfast?" she asked.

"Just toast for me," I said.

"That'll be fine," Padillo said.

"Do you mind if I scrounge an egg or two?" she asked. "I'm famished."

"It's all in the refrigerator."

Padillo followed her into the kitchen and stayed there until she came out with the toast, some more coffee, and bacon and eggs for her. There was a dining area, but we ignored it and used the coffee table.

"We have the meeting at eleven this morning," Padillo told the girl. "I want you to stay here. I want the door locked and bolted. I don't want you to let anyone in but McCorkle or me. No exceptions. If the phone rings, don't answer it."

"When should I expect you back?"

"About three—after we meet with Hardman and the people he's bringing." He looked at his watch and turned to me: "We'd better be going. I left your car in the garage downstairs. You want to use it?"

"We may as well."

"Put the chain lock on when we leave," he told Sylvia. Padillo picked up the black attaché case and we went out. He waited until he heard the lock slide into place.

"That wouldn't stop anyone who really wanted in," I said.

"But it would slow them down long enough for her to get that .25 out of her purse."

The car was running well and I cut down to M Street and turned left, past St. Matthew's Church where they held the services for Kennedy, and then around Scott Circle and under Thomas Circle and down Massachusetts Avenue to Mount Vernon Place and right on Seventh Street. Our progress was slow because of church traffic, but we finally found a place to park in Chinatown and walked back to Seventh.

We climbed the stairs to the shabby office and unlocked the door and went in. It still had its echo of sallow little men talking fast over a battery of telephones. "Try the chair behind the desk," I said. "You can put your feet up."

Padillo placed the attaché case on the desk and tried

my suggestion. I took one of the folding chairs that faced the door. We waited only three minutes until someone knocked. Padillo said come in and it was Magda Shadid. She wore a light wool coat which she took off so we could see her rust-colored knit dress.

"You look beautiful," Padillo told her.

She smiled at him and then at me. "Do you like it? I wore it just for you."

"It accents your best features," he said.

"They're still available for closer inspection."

"I'll keep that in mind."

"And you, Mr. Sad Face, wouldn't you like to be cheered up? You look so sad."

"He's just hung over," Padillo said.

She moved over to me and ran her hand through my hair. "I could cheer you up."

"Watch out. I bite when I'm hung over."

She had extremely dark eyes and if the makeup she used around them was intended to make them seem merry and wicked, it was successful. "That might be interesting," she said, "if you don't bite *too* hard."

"I think you've got the message across, precious," Padillo said. "Why don't you sit down and cross your legs and be decorative."

"It's all so dirty here. Why can't we meet some place that doesn't look like a doss house?"

"For what you're getting paid, you can't complain about the accommodations."

"Paid for what though, Michael?"

"We'll get to that. Tell me, what do you do with all your money?"

"I invest it in Israeli bonds," she said, opened her purse, and took out a cigarette. I let her light her own.

Dymec was the next to arrive. He said hello and sat next to Magda; his large capable hands rested calmly on his knees. He sat straight in the metal chair and gazed at nothing. He seemed to have spent a lot of time waiting and knew not to rush it.

Price was last, arriving a few minutes after Dymec. Padillo had been right. Price was tweedy. He wore a grey and black suit that looked as if it needed a shave, a wide maroon wool tie, and grainy brown brogues with thick soles. He put a plaid hat on one of the vacant chairs as he said hello and sat next to Dymec.

"For the benefit of you two," Padillo said, nodding his head at Magda and Price, "they accepted Dymec as the substitute. They've inspected him and they agreed to the price—seventy-five thousand dollars."

"And we're to get partial payment today," Price said.

"That's right."

Magda dropped her cigarette on the floor and ground it out with her shoe. It was interesting to watch her ankle wiggle. "I believe my portion of seventy-five thousand will be $18,750 which is most generous, considering the fact that I have yet to do anything except meet in shabby offices and listen to your dreary threats. You have never been overly generous in the past, Michael—with anything. I believe I'll have to earn my share. So what do I have to do that's going to be worth that lovely sum?"

"You'll help us get Mrs. McCorkle away from whoever's got her."

"I see. And how do I do that?"

"You walk up to a door, knock on it, and when somebody comes—and they will, because you're a woman—you'll produce a gun and tell them that you wish to see

Mrs. McCorkle. If they don't believe you, you may have to use the gun. Your job will be to get them to open up."

"Do you know where she is?"

"No."

"Then I'm to be your stalking horse."

"Something like that, except you could play a more active role."

"Such as shooting someone."

"You don't have to kill them."

"Just shoot them," she said sweetly.

"That's right."

"For $18,750."

"No. You're forgetting the fourteen thousand. For $32,750—which is a great deal of money for shooting anybody in this country."

"How do you propose to find out where they're keeping his wife?" Dymec asked.

"We're still working on it."

"Any luck?" Price said.

"None so far."

"If you don't find her, what then?" Magda said.

"Then you don't get paid the last half of $18,750. You get the first half for just being on call."

"All right," she said. "I accept."

Padillo turned to her and said in a quick, hard voice: "You're forgetting something, Magda. You're not accepting, you're doing what I tell you to do because you don't have any choice. I could make you do it for nothing, except that I'll pay to keep your efficiency up. When you're free, you tend to get sloppy."

He turned to Price and Dymec. "Before you two start talking about whether you accept or not, what I've told Magda holds true for you both: you're here because I told you to be here. The money is to keep your interest up and to keep you from getting any ideas about pulling a cross."

Price waved a hand as if he were brushing away a lazy fly. "It's all been so vague till now, you know. A chap does wonder a bit."

"All right," Padillo said, "you can quit wondering. Here's how it works: Magda, McCorkle and I will be going after McCorkle's wife while you two pull the fake assassination. We don't know exactly what we'll be doing because we don't know where she is yet. That's the loose part of the operation. It has to be. Your part isn't." He paused and lighted a cigarette.

"The whole point," he continued, "is to get Mrs. McCorkle back. The secondary phase is to expose the Van Zandt crowd to ridicule—to disclose that they paid out seventy-five thousand dollars to have their own Prime Minister shot and that they paid it to con men."

"That's a bit thick," Price said.

"When it doesn't come off," Dymec said, "what do you expect them to do: run down to the Better Business Bureau and file a complaint?"

"Your American is getting better, Dymec."

"Thank you."

"You're going to get cold feet, Dymec."

"Why?"

"Suppose you actually carried out the assassination. What guarantee do you have that you'd get the rest of the money? None. What guarantee do you have that the Africans simply wouldn't tip off the law to start looking for you? If you told the law that they hired you, who'd believe you? Especially you. And what difference would it make?"

He paused again. "So here's what you do, Dymec. You ask them for a letter spelling out the details of their agreement with you. The whole thing. And that letter is to be on their official stationery, signed by Van Zandt, and bearing the official seal. It also has to be witnessed by Boggs and Darragh."

"My God!" Price said.

Dymec looked skeptical. He looked the way I felt. "How would such a letter help?"

"Insurance, man," Price said. "If they wrote a letter stating that they had hired you to assassinate their Prime Minister, that letter would be priceless. Of course they'd pay up to get the letter back."

"They're not that stupid," Dymec said.

"Have they any reason to doubt that you're going to kill Van Zandt?" Padillo said.

Dymec looked at him calmly. He had a fine face for poker. "None."

"All right. You're taking all the risk. You'd like to share a little of it. You'd like to make sure you get paid. When the Prime Minister's paid, they get the letter back."

"I could copy it—there are a number of machines that can do that."

"Not with the official wax seal on it," Padillo said.

"Who keeps the letter?" Dymec said.

"You do, until it's all over."

"I thought you'd have a tricky one, Padillo," Dymec said. "What happens to the letter then?"

"It falls into Price's hands."

"So that's why I'm in," Price said.

"That's right."

"I turn the letter over to my masters and they expose the entire thing."

"Right. The British stand to profit more from this exposure than anyone else. You turn the letter over to them and they create the scandal. It should be a juicy one."

"Who makes the proposition to the Africans?" Dymec said.

"You do."

"What do I tell them?"

"You tell them that we don't believe they're going to release Fredl McCorkle when it's all over and we want some insurance that they will. The letter will do that. They'll get it back when we get Mrs. McCorkle. Second, tell them that you're getting nervous and that you also want some insurance. The letter will do that, too."

"But I get the letter?" Dymec said.

"That's right."

"And then I get it and turn it over to Price who'll make the best use of it."

"Yes."

"Fantastic," Magda said. "Really fantastic. And you say you're not working any longer, Michael?"

"I wouldn't be turning the letter over to the British if I were still working."

"True. But it all still hinges on one thing, doesn't it?"

"That's right."

"And that's on getting Mrs. McCorkle back before the assassination is supposed to take place."

"That's why we want the letter. If we don't find her, they don't do anything to her until they get it back. They'll trade for the letter."

Price got up and started to pace the room. "Let me try to sum it up. I don't mind telling you first of all that this will be quite a feather in my cap."

"I would imagine," Padillo said and I admired the way he kept the sarcasm out of his voice.

"Let me see now: Dymec approaches the Van Zand people. He tells them he wants a letter—to whom it may concern, I suppose—all properly sealed setting forth the fact that one, they have employed him or some unnamed person to assassinate their Prime Minister, and two, that the assassination is to take place on such and such a date at such and such a time at such and such a spot. And three that for the aforementioned services they agree to pay the sum of seventy-five thousand dollars. Have I got it right so far?"

"You're got it right," Padillo said.

"Now then, the reason that they write this letter is that Dymec here is getting a little worried not only about the rest of his commission, but also about what happens to him after it's all over—just in case they have the idea of having him caught in the act, so to speak. And thirdly you and McCorkle are worried about getting Mrs. McCorkle back and she and the letter are considered fair exchange. Of course, once the Prime Minister is assassinated, the letter would be worthless to you because you would implicate yourself in murder."

"That's about it," Padillo said. "If Van Zandt did die and I had the letter, they'd wire me to it."

"Who's they?" I asked.

"My former employers—or Price's present ones."

Price nodded. "Quite. But the assassination does not take place, you somehow rescue Mrs. McCorkle, and turn the letter over to my government who uses it to excoriate Van Zandt and party in the press, the United Nations, and so forth."

"That's it."

"Then all we have to do is get the letter," Dymec said.

"Yes. But you'll have to go through with the entire

charade. You'll have to be up on top of the hotel because they'll have somebody around watching to see that you are. If anything goes wrong, if we don't have Fredl McCorkle safe by the time Van Zandt's car goes by, then I want it. It's all we'll have to get her back."

"But if she is safe?" Dymec asked.

"Then you hand the letter over to Price."

"I'll be at the hotel then?" Price said.

"You'll be on the roof with him."

"Just one thing, Michael dear?" Magda said.

"Yes, precious?"

"Obviously, when this is all over, your African friends aren't going to pay us the rest of the agreed-upon fee. Where will it come from?"

"Out of my own pocket."

"You must have done well in the gun trade."

"It was profitable."

"Speaking of money—" Price said.

Padillo tapped the attaché case. "It's here," he said. He opened the case and tossed each share casually on the table. Then he closed the case, picked it up, and headed for the door. I joined him. "Stay close to your telephones," he told them. "I'll be calling you tonight."

Once again they said nothing, but only nodded, as they kept on counting the money.

— TWENTY —

We walked down the stairs and out of the building and turned south on Seventh Street. When we neared the car, Padillo looked at his watch. "It's too late for breakfast and too early for lunch," he said. "What do you suggest?"

"A drink, except that it's Sunday."

"Don't you know some scoff-law barkeep?"

"Me," I said.

"That'll have to do."

The sermons were still going on as we traveled H Street over to Seventeenth and we missed the post-church traffic. "Let's go by the Roger Smith," Padillo said.

I turned left and drove down to Pennsylvania and then right. "Van Zandt will turn at this corner and the four-car parade will follow the same route we're taking."

Padillo ducked and looked up at the roof garden of the hotel. "It's closed this time of year, you say?"

"That's right."

We turned right on Eighteenth and drove north until it

an into Connecticut Avenue again. I managed to find a
arking place in front of the restaurant. Inside, I switched
n one bank of lights which still left it dark enough to
ave made a flashlight handy. We felt our way to the bar,
umping once into a chair. Padillo went behind the bar
nd switched on the lights that illuminated the sinks and
ottles.

"What are you drinking?" he asked.

"I don't know."

"Martini?"

"Why not."

"Vodka?"

"Gin."

"On the rocks?"

"No."

He mixed the drinks deftly and placed mine before me.
That could help that sad look that Magda wanted to cure."

"I bet she's a lot of fun."

"A swell kid and a peachy dancer."

"Is she good with that gun you were talking about?"

"Very good."

"Is that good enough to go in after Fredl?"

"It is if she's on our team this week."

"Is she?"

"I don't know. That's why you'd better go along."

I nodded. "I was going to suggest it."

Padillo took a sip of his drink. "After you rescue your
ife and drop her off, you can come down to the Roger
mith and lend a hand."

"There'll be a few loose toys still out of the box?"

"A few."

I tried the martini. It was quite good. "Do you think
hey'll write that letter?"

"If Dymec leans on them hard enough. If he sits there with that 'I-won't-budge-till-you-do' stare of his, they'll probably give it to him. They won't have much choice."

"It's insurance for him."

"He'd better think so. Of course, he could just simply tell them what we want to use it for."

"I thought of that," I said. "But there's not as much percentage in it for him."

"Let's hope so. I also hope that it gets Price off my neck."

"It shows," I said, "but I've never known you to be so considerate of people who shoot at you."

Padillo held up the cocktail shaker and looked at it. "I'm not really. Let's have one more and then have some lunch."

"All right."

He mixed the drinks and poured them. "Funny about Price," he said.

"How?"

"He wants the letter, but that alone won't keep him off my back."

"What else?"

"How many times did he shoot at me last night?"

"Twice."

"He missed twice. Five years ago he wouldn't have missed once. Three years ago he would have been dead if he had. You notice I didn't shoot back."

"I took it for a sporting gesture."

Padillo grinned. "Not quite. My hand was shaking too much."

We walked over to Harvey's on Connecticut Avenue and had lunch there which was no better nor worse than the lunches they had been serving for the past 108 years. Afterwards, we drove back to Seventh Street, found a parking place, and climbed the stairs to the office with the folding steel chairs and the dust-covered desk. I asked Padillo how his side was and when he said it bothered him I offered him the chair behind the desk. I turned another chair around so that it would serve as a footrest and we sat there in the drab office on a Sunday afternoon and waited for the gangster men to arrive.

They arrived on time, at two p.m. Hardman brought them in, three Negroes of different shades of brown, all dressed in quiet, conservative dark suits, white shirts, muted ties and highly-polished shoes. He introduced us to them and then told us who they were.

"This is Johnny Jay," he said of a tall, thin man with dark skin, a bleak look, and wide mouth with thick rubbery lips. He looked to be about thirty-one or two. He nodded at us, took out a handkerchief, dusted off one of the folding chairs, and sat down.

"This here's Tulip," Hardman said, indicating a man with a dark pitted face, a wide, stocky build, and curiously delicate-looking hands that flitted around like thick butterflies, lighting first on his lapels, then down to check the flaps on his jacket pockets, then the trouser pockets, then up to his head to smooth a hair back into place, and then to the knot of his blue and maroon striped tie.

The last man that Hardman introduced was a mulatto, a sleek-skinned, handsome lad whom he called Nineball. Nineball wore a double-breasted suit of dark grey flannel, a white shirt with a tab collar, neatly knotted green and black foulard tie, and a well-clipped mustache. He wore them all well and gave us a friendly smile when Hardman mentioned his name.

"These the men you gonna be workin with," Hardman told them. "They also the men who gonna pay you two thousand dollars to do whatever needs to be done like I told you, and I don't want no mess-ups."

"I'll have the money for you first thing in the morning," I said. "As soon as the banks open."

Hardman took out his ostrich billfold and opened it so he could read something he had written on a notepad.

"Gonna cost you $10,247 for the whole thing. Six big ones for my three friends here, a thousand each to rent the moving van and the pickup, a thousand into the hip pocket of the man at the phone company to get them phones in first thing in the morning, a thousand to get the two cars painted, and $247 for expenses like uniforms and a couple of other items."

Nineball spoke up. "We gonna have to zap anybody?"

"Not if we can help it," Padillo said.

Nineball nodded and said: "But it just possibly might be necessary."

"It possibly might," Padillo said.

"How you got it planned now?" Hardman asked.

"There's one thing about those figures you were reeling off," I said.

"What?" Hardman said.

"There's no cut for you."

"We get around to that later."

Padillo leaned forward from his chair behind the desk and rested his arms on the blotter. I noticed that he had dusted it off. "It works like this," he said. "You'll be outside the trade mission on Massachusetts Avenue by eleven-thirty on Tuesday morning. You'll be parked so that you have a clear view of the house. If there's a rear entrance, whoever's in the big truck will cover that. At precisely eleven-thirty a young white girl will go into the trade mission. She'll be driving a new green Chevrolet with D.C. plates. At eleven-thirty you'll start your four-way conference call. I assume that Hardman's going to be in the pickup so he'll originate the call. If that girl's not out of that place by noon, you go and bring her out."

He waited. There were no questions. Hardman cleared his throat and said: "I've told em about that part, baby. I also mentioned that there'd be a bonus in it if they gotta go in."

"That's right," Padillo said.

"Who's gonna be drivin my car?" Hardman said.

"McCorkle. The woman you met at Betty's will be with him."

"Uh-huh."

"McCorkle will be parked a couple of blocks away from the mission on a side street. When that girl is brought out of the mission, both the pickup and the moving van will follow whatever car they take her in to wherever they take her. McCorkle will be following a block or two behind. You'll be telling him where you're going by means of the conference call."

Padillo paused and lighted a cigarette and offered them around. Nobody took one. "When the car that has the girl arrives at wherever it's going, you'll wait until they take her in—I'm guessing it will be they—and come out and leave. Then McCorkle here and the woman will move up to the door—"

"You don't know what kind of door yet?" Tulip asked.

"We don't even know what section of town it'll be in," Padillo said. "But the woman and McCorkle will move up to the door of whatever it is. They'll be looking as much as possible like new tenants who are accompanied by their movers—you four."

"Uh-huh," Hardman said.

"The woman will ring the bell or knock on the door or whatever. When it's opened, you move up behind them fast because that's when you go in."

"They gonna let us in like that?" Nineball asked. "Just cause she asks them to?"

"She's not gonna ask them, baby," Hardman said. "You ain't seen this little old gal. She's gonna have a gun aimed right at that mother's belly. Right, Mac?"

"Right," I said.

"When you're inside," Padillo went on, "your main job will be to get Mrs. McCorkle and the girl out safely and fast."

"You talking about that little old gal we followed there now," Hardman said. "You ain't talking about the one who's handling the gun."

"No. Mrs. McCorkle and Sylvia Underhill are the ones who have to get out fast. The other one can usually take care of herself."

"And in this house, that we don't know where it is, will be where the trouble is?" Johnny Jay said.

"That's right. That'll be the trouble."

"Whatta we do with the women after it's over?" Nineball asked.

"Take em to Betty's," Hardman said. "Then you hang around a while outside, make sure nobody's comin in after em."

Hardman looked around the room. "You got any questions, you better ask them now." They looked at him, their faces impassive. Hardman rose. "O.K., I'll be in touch with you later this afternoon," he told them. "You got things to do so you might as well get doing them."

They got up and nodded at us as they filed out of the room. Hardman watched them leave, then turned to Padillo and me.

"They O.K.?" he asked.

"They look fine," I said.

Padillo nodded.

"Where you gonna be, baby, while all this fun's going on?"

"At the hotel," Padillo said.

"You mentioned Mush yesterday."

"He's going to be with me—if that's O.K."

"Sure," Hardman said. "I told him to expect something. You know exactly what you gonna need him for yet?"

"Not yet."

"Uh-huh. Mush come pretty high."

"If he's as good as he thinks he is, I'll pay it."

"You wanta make your own deal with him?"

"It's up to you. What's your cut?"

Hardman studied the floor for a moment. "Just make the whole package fifteen thousand. I'll take whatever's left over."

"Then I'll make my own deal with Mush. I'd like to see him tonight."

"Where at?" Hardman said.

"My hotel—he's been there before."

"What time about?"

"About nine."

"He be there."

Hardman rose from his chair and moved to the door. "You reckon this'll about do it?"

Padillo nodded. "Keep in touch."

"I aim to."

"The money will be ready in the morning," I said.

He waved his huge hand. "I'll pick it up around noon and come by for lunch."

"It'll be on the house."

Hardman laughed. "I was countin on that." He waved goodbye and left and his 240-odd pounds seemed to shake the building as he bounded down the steps.

Padillo stared at the desk blotter until Hardman's footsteps couldn't be heard any more and then he said: "You trust him, huh?"

"What am I supposed to say: 'With my life?'"

"I don't know. We've been talking some awfully big money and he's putting in an awfully small chit."

"Maybe he's got something else in mind."

Padillo quit staring at the desk blotter and looked at me. "Maybe," he said. "If he does, you're going to have fun on Tuesday when you have to decide whether you like the way his mind works."

— TWENTY-ONE —

We drove back through the slow Sunday afternoon traffic to my apartment, where we put the car into the basement garage and took the elevator up to the floor where I lived. I rang the chimes and when there was no response I unlocked the door and opened it as far as the chain would permit.

"It's all right, Sylvia," I said. "You can let us in."

I closed the door so she could take the chain off and we went in. She had cleaned things up: The pillows were fluffed, the ashtrays were empty, the dirty dishes and cups were out of sight, presumably in the dishwasher. I didn't look, but I was sure that the beds had been made. She was earning her keep.

"How did your meetings go?" she asked.

"All right," Padillo said. "They understand what they have to do."

"Is it the same as we talked about?"

"Yes."

"Would you like some coffee?"

"I would," I said. Padillo said he would, too.

She brought two cups in and we sat in the livingroom and drank them. I had always liked Sundays in that apartment with Fredl. They were quiet, lazy days littered with *The New York Times*, *The Washington Post*, and *The Washington Star* and built around long, large breakfasts with endless cups of coffee. If we got up early enough, I would turn on the radio to a semi-country music station that played a full hour of uninterrupted fundamentalist hymns. Fredl got so that she could harmonize fairly well with "Farther Along" and "Wreck on the Highway." Later, I would switch to WGMS and she would read me the cattier comments from the Washington papers' society columns and add her own observations about those whose names were making news. On fine afternoons she sometimes would drag me out for a good German walk or, if it were raining, we might go to the Circle Theater and watch a double feature of bad old movies and eat a half-gallon of buttered popcorn. There were other variations of Sunday, equally prosaic, equally unplanned. Sometimes we just read or wandered around the National Gallery. Once in a while we would take the air-shuttle up to New York and walk around Manhattan, have a couple of drinks and early dinner, and fly back. Sundays were ours, unshared, and we had grown fond of them. I found myself not caring much for this particular Sunday. I found myself missing my wife and worrying about where she was and what she was doing and how she felt. I found myself feeling useless and futile and not overly bright.

"When do I get to hit somebody?" I asked Padillo.

"Edgy?"

"It's growing. Maybe I should bite on a bullet."

"There's no cure," he said.

"What do you do?"

"To keep from screaming?"

"Yes."

"I make silent yells."

"Does it help?"

"Not much."

"It doesn't sound as if it would."

"But it takes a while to figure out how to do it."

"What's scheduled for the rest of the afternoon—or is this free time?"

"Nothing scheduled."

I rose. "I think I'll take a nap. A nightmare would be better than this."

Padillo looked at me and frowned. "You're still calling it. You can bring in the law."

"I've thought about it, but I think we've gone too far. I'm not even sure they'd believe us. I'm not even sure that I do."

"You can still do it up until tomorrow," he said. "After that it'll probably be too late."

"If I'd called in the cops, Fredl would be dead now. This way she's still alive. But the odds seem to be shifting. It's getting complicated and tricky and too many people are in on it. Why not get a few more? Why not just call the FBI, tell them to put some of their bright young men on Darragh and Boggs, find out where Fredl is, and go in and get her? That sounds simple. It sounds easy. Just a phone call. It sounds so easy that there must be something wrong with it."

"Not much," Padillo said. "First they'd have to take you in and you'd have to answer a few questions. You could tell them about Darragh and Boggs and Van Zandt.

That would be a little tricky, because they have diplomatic immunity, but the FBI could check it all out—in maybe twenty-four hours or so. Then you could tell them about Magda and Price and Dymec and they could check that out—whether they're double agents or not. My ex-employers would be glad to let them know within a week or so. Then there's Hardman and Mush and that crowd. You could tell the cops about Hardman. They know a lot already, but you could tell them more. Hardman and Mush wouldn't mind, except that they might get a little miffed at you. Not much. Just enough so that you'd keep looking over your shoulder for a long time to come. And during all this, Fredl is sitting out there with a kill order on her that's probably set on an hour-to-hour basis with a deadline for sometime around Tuesday afternoon. But you're right. You might be able to get her out with help. And then both of you would be around for a week to enjoy the reunion."

"Who would it be?"

"You can almost take your choice," Padillo said. "I'd bet first on the Africans and then on Dymec and Price. Hardman's people would get a high rating, too. You know too much and you're in too deep, Mac."

"They would remember," Sylvia said. "Darragh and Boggs—all of them. I know what kind of memories they have."

I sighed. "I said it was too simple. All of my ideas are too simple, but that's because I've tried to live an uncomplicated life in a world full of nuts. I should know better. I thought that selling food and drink would be simple, but I should have known better about that, too. You have a full house and you turn somebody away and they turn out to be the parents of Jesus Christ." I got up and headed for the bedroom. "Pound on the door around six," I said. "Maybe I'll be tired of my nightmare by then."

The bed was still too large, but I surprised myself and fell off to sleep quickly. I dreamed about Fredl as I expected, but it was a pleasant dream. We were on a canoe floating down a crystal stream on a warm June day and I was enjoying myself because I didn't have to paddle too hard. We were having a fine time and I was sorry when the knocking on the door woke me up.

I washed my face and brushed my teeth and went back into the livingroom. My watch said it was eight o'clock and only Sylvia was there. She was sitting on the couch, her feet tucked up under her.

"Where's Padillo?"

"He went back to the hotel. He has to meet someone there at nine."

"Mush."

"Are you hungry?" she asked.

"I don't think so."

"May I get you anything?"

"No, thank you. Why did you let me sleep so long?"

"He said it would help you pass the time. He called it fast time."

We sat there talking about not very much for an hour or so. Sylvia made some sandwiches and we ate those and then the phone rang. It was nine-thirty.

I said hello and it was Boggs. "We have decided to give Dymec the letter," he said. "It was not a unanimous decision. I was against it."

"It's a good thing you lost. Is my wife there?"

"Yes. But don't try to make any more stipulations, McCorkle."

"I didn't make them. Dymec made them. He's getting nervous. I don't think he trusts you very much and I didn't do anything to discourage him because I don't trust you at all. Put my wife on."

"If anything happens to that letter—"

"I know," I said. "You've made your case often enough."

"I'll make it again. Nothing must happen to that letter."

"Tell Dymec that. He'll have it."

"I've told him."

"When will he get it?"

"Tuesday."

"All right. Let me talk to my wife."

"You'll talk to her when I'm quite through. The person who has this letter could conceivably sell it for a large sum. If this Dymec has any such idea, I suggest that you dissuade him."

"He wants the letter because he doesn't trust you. We want it because we don't trust you. You don't want us to have it because you don't trust us. I'm the new boy on the block and I don't know too much about this kind of business, but it seems to be built on mutual distrust and unless each side has its low leverage, then the whole deal's likely to go up in smoke. That letter is our leverage—and Dymec's leverage."

"Let nothing happen to it," Boggs said. "Here is your wife."

"Fredl?"

"I'm here, darling. I'm all right and please try not to—"

They cut her off. I was supposed to tip her off that we would try to break her out on Tuesday. I couldn't see how I could tip her off with only a word or two. It didn't leave much room for the secret code. I replaced the phone, then picked it up again, and dialed a number. I gave the operator Padillo's room and he answered.

"I just heard from Boggs," I said. "He'll give Dymec the letter."

"Did you talk to Fredl?"

"Yes."

"Is she all right?"

"Yes, but I can't tip her off. They don't give me enough time."

"What did Boggs have to say?"

"We lied to each other about mutual trust. Dymec seems to be playing the letter straight with them."

"I thought he would," Padillo said. "It gives him a handle in case they get cute after it's over."

"What now?" I said.

"Mush just left. He's getting the Winchester for Dymec."

"You know what you're going to do yet?"

"Most of it," he said. "It depends on Price and Dymec and Magda. It still depends on who decides to jump where. I think I know."

"Anything more for me tonight?"

"I don't think so. I'll call the trio and tell them it's set. That'll give them the rest of the night and most of tomorrow to decide whose throat should be cut."

"I'll keep Sylvia here," I said.

"That's best. Say goodnight to her for me."

"I will. I'll be down at the bar around ten tomorrow. That early enough?"

"Fine," he said. "I'll see you then."

I hung up the phone and turned to Sylvia. She was looking at me with her lips slightly parted, her brown eyes wide as if she thought that she might have been remembered in the will, but wasn't really expecting too much.

"Padillo said to tell you goodnight."

"Anything else?"

"Just that it would be best for you to stay here tonight."

"That isn't much, is it?" she said.

"I wouldn't expect more."

"No, I suppose I really shouldn't."

There wasn't a great deal else for me to say so I went over to the bar and mixed a Scotch-and-water. Sylvia said she didn't want one.

"You know him very well, don't you?"

"Padillo?"

"Yes."

"I know him fairly well."

"Doesn't he ever need anyone?"

"Like you?"

"Yes. Like me, damn it."

"I don't know. You'll have to ask him."

"I did ask him."

"What did he say?"

She was silent for a moment and when she spoke she seemed to be speaking to her hands which rested in her lap. "He said he didn't have any more time to be lonely—that his time for being lonely had run out years ago."

"What else did he say?"

"Something I'm not sure I understand."

"What?"

"He said that he casts a yellow shadow. What does that mean?"

"It's what the Arabs say, I think. It means he carries a lot of luck around. All bad."

"Does he?"

"For others. For those who get too close."

"I don't believe in luck," she said.

"That's funny," I said. "Neither does Padillo."

— TWENTY-TWO —

I met Padillo at the saloon the next morning at ten and we spent an hour doing some work that needed to be done if we were to continue in the business of selling liquor and food to people who already bought too much of both. We went over some invoices and Padillo made a couple of suggestions that would probably save us a thousand or so a year. We called in Herr Horst and talked about a waiter who kept forgetting to come to work.

"I believe he drinks," Herr Horst said, and added: "Secretly."

"It's not much of a secret if you know about it," Padillo said.

"He's a good waiter," I said. "Give him one more chance, but tell him that's just what it is."

"It won't do any good," Padillo said.

"It makes me feel like a humanitarian."

"I shall speak to him," Herr Horst said. "Again."

We discussed the week's menu, decided to give a new

wholesale produce dealer a try, went over the merits of two employee health and hospital insurance programs and decided on one, and agreed to run some small space advertisements in a concert program. It was more work than I had done in a week.

Herr Horst left and sent us in some coffee by a busboy. Padillo sat behind the desk of the office; I sat on the couch.

"How's your side?" I asked.

"Better, but I should get the bandage changed before tomorrow."

"You want the doctor?"

"No. I'll let Sylvia do it."

"She'll like that. She wants to do things for you."

"She'll make someone a good wife."

"I think she's been writing 'Mrs. Michael Padillo' just to see how nice it looks."

"I'm too old or she's too young or both."

"She thinks you're in your prime."

"I passed that ten years ago. I was an early bloomer. Now it's only a few years away from one of those places with planned leisure activities."

"She's a nice kid; you could do worse."

Padillo lighted a cigarette. "That's right. I could, Mac, but she couldn't."

He got up and walked over to the grey steel file and pulled a drawer open. He looked into it, seemed to find nothing that was interesting, closed it, and opened the second drawer. It was the absentminded, aimless action of someone who is thinking of other things.

"Let's take a walk," he said, and abruptly closed the file drawer.

"Are we going somewhere or is it just a nice day?"

"We'll pay a visit to the roof garden of the Roger Smith."

"All right."

We told Herr Horst that we would be back and walked over to Eighteenth and up to K Street and down past where Mr. Kiplinger writes his newsletter, and crossed a street to the Roger Smith Hotel which rises eleven stories above the corner of Eighteenth and Pennsylvania Avenue. The United States Information Agency is just across the street at its faintly patriotic address of 1776 Pennsylvania.

There are Roger Smith hotels in other towns such as Stamford, Connecticut, White Plains and New Brunswick. They cater to the tourist and the person who travels on a limited expense account. In Washington, visitors like the hotel because it's only a block and a half from the White House and the rates are reasonable even during the Cherry Blossom Festival.

We took the automatic elevator to the tenth floor, got out, and walked up a flight of stairs to some French doors that were fastened with a hook and eye. We undid that and stepped out onto the roof garden. On the Pennsylvania Avenue side a curved blue metal shield formed a shell for the orchestra which played for the dancers on summer evenings. The dance floor was of marble and chairs were stacked against the cube-like part of the roof which housed the elevator works. From the chest-high cement railing that ran around the roof you could look down Pennsylvania and see the grey mass of the Executive Office Building which once was considered plenty large enough for the State Department as well as the entire military establishment—now bursting the seams of the Pentagon.

Everything was painted red and yellow and blue on the roof and it had the air of a party that had come to an unpleasant end. Padillo and I leaned on the cement railing and looked down the avenue.

"It would be an easy job," he said. There was a clear view to Seventeenth and Pennsylvania where Van Zandt's car would make its turn. The cement bannister would even provide a convenient gun rest.

"Has he looked it over?" I asked.

"Dymec?"

"Yes."

"He came up yesterday. I talked to him last night after Mush brought him the rifle."

"What does he have?"

"What he wanted. The Winchester model 70."

"Why did he want it so early?"

"His real reason is probably that he wants to zero it in. The excuse he gave me is that he wants to decide how to conceal it when he brings it up here."

"Have you figured out how you're going to stop him?"

Padillo looked down at the avenue again. "I think so," he said. "It depends on what happens tomorrow when you go after Fredl."

"Have you arranged where everybody meets tomorrow?"

Padillo leaned against the rail and nodded. "Hardman picks you and Magda up at eleven. Then you, the pickup and the moving van follow Sylvia out to the trade mission. Mush and I will be moving around in his car—in this general area. Price waits in the lobby from two until Dymec goes up to the roof."

"That'll be around two-thirty."

"The official tour leaves the trade mission at two. You'll go in after Fredl and Sylvia around one-thirty, I'd say. That should give you time to get down here."

"You want anyone else to come with me—Hardman?"

"No."

I looked at my watch. "I have to go to the bank. Hardman's coming by for lunch—and for the money."

"O.K. I wired Zurich yesterday. They'll transfer some funds. They should be here tomorrow."

We walked down the stairs to the tenth floor and took the elevator down. We caught a cab to my bank. I wrote out the check and winced at its size and then took it over to a vice-president so that I could get it cashed without fuss. He didn't like to see that much money go out, but he got it rounded up and handed it to me in a thick manilla envelope.

"Real estate transaction, Mr. McCorkle?" he asked knowingly.

"The cards were bad," I said and walked away from the thoughtful look that appeared on his face.

"You can ride shotgun," I told Padillo and we walked back to the restaurant. Hardman was waiting for us in the office. "Sorry I'm late," I told him and handed over the envelope.

He undid the clasp and looked inside and said, "my, my" and stuck the envelope in the wide pocket of his camel's hair polo coat.

"Can't stay for lunch, baby," he said. "Too many things moving."

"Got time for a drink?"

"Make time for that."

I picked up the phone and ordered three martinis. "You want Scotch?" I asked Hardman.

He shook his head. "Martini's fine."

"Phones going in O.K.?" Padillo asked him.

"Man's working on em right now."

"When will he be through?"

Hardman looked at his watch. "Couple of hours—about three'd put us on the safe side."

"Can we set up a trial conference call for four?"

"Don't see why not. Lemme think. That'd be my car, Mush's, and the pickup and the van."

"Right."

"Mush and I'll pick you up where?"

Padillo looked at me. I shrugged. "Mac's apartment," e said. "We'll be outside at four."

"Be there," Hardman assured us.

The drinks came and Hardman told us what he had been oing. The pickup and the van had been painted; he'd got our white sets of coveralls; the phones were going in, and ulip, Johnny Jay, and Nineball were staying sober. We vent over the time that he should pick Magda and me up e next morning and he said that he had it all straight.

We finished the drinks and followed Hardman out into e restaurant. He left and we moved over to the bar and atched the customers get rid of their weekend hangovers. said hello to some regulars and introduced Padillo. We tayed at the restaurant until three-thirty and then went to ny apartment. I opened the door with a key and then waited or Sylvia to take the chain off the lock.

"Quiet day?" I said.

"Very quiet," she said.

"Nervous?" Padillo asked.

"Only a little."

"We have to go out for a while but then we'll come ack and keep you company the rest of the day," he said.

At four Padillo and I went downstairs and waited for ardman and Mush. They were on time and I got into ardman's Cadillac and Padillo went in Mush's Buick. Ve drove to the corner and the Buick turned right. Hardman turned left. He picked up the telephone that hung from his dashboard and signaled the operator. He drove with his left hand and held the phone to his ear with his right.

"This is YR 4-7896. I want to set up a conference call with the following numbers." He read off three more numbers with the YR prefix. "That's right, operator, soon as possible."

He hung up the phone and we drove on, heading towards Georgetown.

"We going any place in particular?" I asked.

"Just cruisin," he said. "Any place special you wanna go?"

I couldn't think of any place and told him so.

We were on Wisconsin Avenue heading north towards Nebraska when the telephone buzzed. Hardman picked it up and said: "This is YR 4-7896. Thanks, operator." He handed the phone to me. "She says the call's ready. Tell em who you are and where you are."

"This is McCorkle on Wisconsin and T," I said. "We're heading north."

"This is Padillo. We're on Connecticut and S. Streets, heading north."

"This is Tulip. We're on Georgia and Kennedy Streets, heading south."

"This is Johnny Jay at Fourteenth and Columbia Road. We turnin on to Fourteenth and heading south."

"Hold on," I said and turned to Hardman. "They're all coming in fine."

"Tell em to keep talking and to meet us at Nebraska and Military Road in twenty minutes," he said.

"That's going to take some driving for a couple of them."

"That's what they paid to do."

"Meet us at Nebraska and Military Road in twenty minutes. That will be four-forty p.m. Let me know if you've got it."

"This is Padillo. I understand. We're heading there now."

"This is Johnny Jay. Shit, man, I'm gonna have to fly."

"This is Tulip. I'll be there."

"They've got it," I told Hardman.

"Tell em not to hang up."

"Don't hang up—keep the call going."

We drove down Wisconsin and turned right on Nebraska. We hit a long red light at Connecticut, crossed and drove slowly down Nebraska until we got to Military Road. A white moving van drove past us, followed by a white pickup truck. Both had "Four-Square Moving Company" painted on their doors. Mush's Buick turned out of a side street. He waved at us and I waved back.

Hardman reached for the phone. "All right," he said. "We can knock off now. Take em back where you got em." He signaled the operator and told her the call was through.

"They seem to work fine," I said. "They'll be fine tomorrow."

He drove me back to my apartment. "Anything else tonight?" he asked.

"I don't think so."

"See you in the morning then."

"Where'll you be if something comes up?"

"This phone or Betty's."

"O.K. See you tomorrow."

I waited until Mush drove up and let Padillo out and we rode up the elevator together. Inside the apartment, Sylvia put a new bandage on Padillo, I mixed three drinks, and we turned on the television set and watched the six-thirty news. There was nothing about Van Zandt.

At seven Padillo telephoned Magda Shadid, Philip Price, and Jon Dymec. He gave them their final instructions in brief, concise sentences.

He came back to the couch and sat down next to Sylvia. "Did you call the police today?" he asked.

"Yes."

"They have anything?"

"No. They're still unable to locate the car that struck Dad."

"Did they want you to do anything else?"

"No. When I was there I made arrangements to have him sent home." She said it without faltering.

"Are your people expecting to hear from you?"

"I sent a cable to mother and charged it to this telephone. I have the charges," she said to me. "I'll repay you."

"Forget it."

"Do you still have that automatic?" Padillo asked her.

"Yes."

"Take it with you tomorrow. Can you hide it some place—in your brassiere or something?"

She flushed slightly. "Or something. Will I need it?"

"I don't know," he said. "I just want you to have it."

The telephone rang and I answered it.

"You can talk to your wife, McCorkle." It was Boggs. "Fredl?"

"I'm on now, darling."

"Are you all right?"

"Yes, I'm fine. I'm just getting so tired and I—"

They cut her off again. Boggs came back on. "Is Padillo there?" he asked.

"Yes."

"Is everything ready for tomorrow? You have the correct times?"

"We have everything," I said.

"Well," he said and his voice trailed off. For once he seemed at a loss for something to say. "I don't suppose I should wish you good luck," he said finally.

"I don't think so."

"Yes, well—goodnight then."

I hung up the phone.

"Boggs," I said.

"Fredl all right?"

"Yes. I suppose so. She's tired."

"What did Boggs want?"

"He wanted to know whether he should wish us good luck."

— TWENTY-THREE —

The alarm rang at eight Tuesday morning and I turned it off and put my cigarette out on the big ceramic tray that was on the night table next to the bed. The tray had thirty-seven butts in it. I had counted them twenty minutes earlier. I had awakened at three and for a while just stared up into the darkness until I knew that sleep was at an end and that I had five hours to spend with myself. The prospect of my company was never less pleasing. I was a bore. I talked too much and listened too little. I was opinionated and self-indulgent. I had no insight, but plenty of self-pity. I had a tendency to blame others for the mistakes I made. I was growing old. I drank too much.

On that I lighted another cigarette and got up and went into the bathroom and brushed my teeth again and drank a glass of water and stared into the mirror for a while. I didn't see anyone I wanted to know so I went back into the bedroom and turned on the high-intensity lamp, picked up volume two of Mr. Pepys's diary, and tried to get interested in how he was making out with the chambermaid. After fifteen minutes my mind wandered and I put the book aside. I lay in the bed and smoked another cigarette in fearless defiance of all rules of health and personal safety. I stared up at the ceiling with the light on and after a while I tried it with the light off. It didn't make much difference.

The time passed that way, neither slower nor faster than usual, half in the dark, half in the light, and by the time the alarm rang, it was done and I had battled through another night without resorting to Dr. Sinatra's prescription of whatever it takes—pills, prayer or a bottle of Jack Daniels.

I got dressed more slowly than usual because I felt a decade or two older than usual and went into the living-room where Padillo was sitting on the couch drinking a cup of coffee and smoking a cigarette that he didn't seem to enjoy. I said "uh" and he came back with a snappy "guh" and I went on into the kitchen and poured water on top of a teaspoon of instant coffee.

After the first cup, I tried a second.

"That belly gun," Padillo said by way of greeting.

"Uh-huh."

"You have any rounds for it?"

"No."

"Here." He took out a box of .38 shells and put six on the coffee table. I got up and went into the bedroom and got the gun out of my topcoat pocket. I came back and picked up the shells from the table, flipped the cylinder open, and loaded it, just like they used to do at the Criterion Theater on Saturday afternoon.

"You don't think I'll need any more than six?"

"If you need more than six, it really won't matter."

Sylvia Underhill came in and said good morning an asked if we would like her to prepare some breakfast an we said no. She was wearing ivory pumps and a woole suit of periwinkle blue that had a nubby weave. She smile at both of us, but Padillo got a little extra in his, and I started wondering when someone would smile at me lik that again. She looked pretty and smart and very young– not at all as if she were going out to badger the membe of a trade mission.

After her breakfast and more coffee for Padillo and m we went over what each of us was supposed to do. I gre more nervous each time we went over it, but Padillo an Sylvia discussed the steps as if they were planning Fu Night at the Elks' Club. We went over it until I came dow with a fit of yawning and then we stopped.

"White night?" Padillo asked.

"Close to it."

He looked at his watch. "Magda should be here shortly.

We waited some more. Sylvia was on the couch wit her feet tucked under her. She held a cup and saucer. Sh had held them for twenty minutes. Padillo was at the othe end of the couch. He was slumped back, his head restin against the cushions, his feet stretched out before him an crossed at the ankles. He smoked cigarettes and blew ring at the ceiling. When he wasn't smoking, his mouth we into a line so thin that he didn't seem to have any lips. sat in an easy chair, my favorite one, and gnawed at hangnail because it gave me something to do and becaus it was the most constructive thing I had done all mornin

The chimes rang at ten-forty-five and I got up, crosse the room, and opened the door. It was Magda Shadid an she was dressed for anything that one might have enoug money to take her to at that time of the morning. Ther was a dark grey coat that felt like cashmere when she turned so that it could fall into my hands. Underneath the coat she was wearing a white and grey dress whose pattern was made up of large inverted V's. The dress seemed to have been applied with care, layer by layer, handrubbed possibly, and no one could say that it wouldn't have been pleasant work.

"Mr. McCorkle," she said sweetly. "You look very tired this morning."

"Thank you."

"Hello, Michael, how are you? Grim and morose as usual, I see. And this must be—not Mrs. McCorkle, surely?"

"No," Padillo said. "Magda Shadid, Sylvia Underhill."

"How do you do," Sylvia said.

"And what do you do for my very old friend Michael?"

"She leads and we follow," I said.

Magda gracefully eased into one of the chairs, crossed her legs, and began to take off her gloves. She took them off carefully, and spent time loosening each finger.

"Then you know where Mrs. McCorkle is?" she said.

"Not yet, precious, but we will. Mac will explain it to you along the way."

"Would you like some coffee?" Sylvia asked.

"I'd love some. Black, please, with loads of sugar."

Sylvia rose and went into the kitchen.

"You always had an eye for the young ones, Michael, but I never knew you to make use of children."

"She's twenty-one," Padillo said. "When you were twenty-one you were running three agents out of Munich, until you sold them piecemeal to Gehlen."

"It was a hard winter. Besides, my sweet, I'm European. There's such a difference."

225

"Such," Padillo agreed.

Sylvia came back in with the coffee. "That's a stunnin suit," Magda told her. "Have you known Michael long?

"Not long," Sylvia said, "and the suit cost ten pound six off the peg—that's about thirty dollars."

"Closer to twenty-nine," Magda said. "I should war you Michael has a way of using his friends—especiall his old friends—that is sometimes quite disconcerting Have you discovered this yet, Miss Underhill?"

"No, but then I don't have all the years necessary t make me an old friend, do I?"

I gave that round to Sylvia on points and said: "Whe is Hardman due?"

"Any minute," Padillo said.

"I take his Cadillac and Magda goes with me, right? I said it for the benefit of Magda. We had gone over it dozen times.

"That's it."

The telephone rang and I answered it. It was Hardman "I'm about ten minutes away from your house, Mac, an I'm starting the conference call now."

"Where's Mush?"

"Right behind me."

"And the trucks?"

"Big one's already headin out there. Pickup's right be hind Mush."

"We'll be downstairs in ten minutes," I said.

"See you."

I hung up the phone and told them to get ready. I wer into my bedroom and took a topcoat out of the closet. put the revolver in its righthand pocket, picked up th knife from the dresser, snicked open the blade, felt th point to see if it was still sharp, closed it, and dropped into the left-hand coat pocket. It would come in handy if someone had a string-wrapped package to open. We took the elevator down to the lobby where Magda, Padillo and I got off. Sylvia stayed on to continue down to the basement garage where her car was parked. Padillo turned just as he left the elevator and looked at her. She smiled—or tried to. He nodded his head. I couldn't see whether he smiled or not.

"Take care, kid," he said.

"You, too."

The elevator door closed and the three of us walked through the plate-glass doors that opened on to the curved driveway. We waited only two or three minutes before Hardman's Cadillac rolled up. It was a Coupe de Ville and long enough to satisfy anyone's status cravings. Hardman was dressed in white coveralls with "Four-Square Movers" stitched in red thread across the back. The coveralls made him enormous. The Buick, driven by Mush, rolled up behind the Cadillac. The white pickup truck stopped at the curb. Tulip was driving.

"Keys in the car," Hardman said to me. "Conference call's gone through and everybody's on."

"O.K.," I said. "You follow the girl's Chevrolet. She should be coming out any minute."

"We'll be right behind her. Truck's going to be in the alley."

I opened the door for Magda and she got in. I walked around to the other side. Padillo was just getting into the Buick next to Mush. "Stay in touch," he said.

"Don't worry."

I started the Cadillac, put the automatic gear into drive, checked the brakes, discovered I had power steering, and drove out into the street. Sylvia, driving the green Chevrolet, pulled out of the basement garage and the white pickup with Tulip at the wheel and Hardman beside him fell in behind her. I looked at my watch. It was eleven fifteen. I picked up the phone and said hello. Padillo answered. He said: "Everybody check in."

"I'm right behind the pickup," I said. "We're heading up Twentieth to Massachusetts."

"This is Hardman. We right behind Missy's Chevvy On Twentieth, heading for Massachusetts."

"This Johnny Jay," another voice came in. "Tulip's drivin. We in the van and moving up Mass bout five minutes away from where we supposed to be."

"All right," Padillo said. "Hardman will serve as talker from now on. If he says move, you'll move. It's all yours, Hardman."

The big man's bass voice rumbled over the telephone. "I'll give it to you as we go . . . turnin left on Massachusetts . . . now we're at Sheridan Circle . . . we around the circle and straight on Mass . . . now we two blocks past the circle and about six blocks or so from where we're goin . . ."

I drove with my left hand on the wheel and held the phone with my right. Magda leaned against the door and stared out through the windshield.

"Three blocks from where we're goin," Hardman said.

At the end of that block I turned right, then left into a driveway, backed up, and drove the Cadillac to the corner and parked it just in front of a stop sign. I could see Massachusetts Avenue traffic for two blocks each way. I cut the engine, lighted a cigarette, and kept listening to the telephone.

"Missy's lookin for a place to park," Hardman's voice said. "She's found one bout a block away . . . She's parked

O.K. . . . Now she's gettin out and headin back for the place . . . Come in, Johnny Jay."

"We right behind the house we supposed to be behind," Johnny Jay's voice said. "No action."

"All right," Hardman said. "It's eleven-thirty now . . . Missy's goin up to the door . . . She's ringin the bell . . . Me and Tulip's parked right in front across the street in a no-parkin zone . . . Man's openin the door—thin white cat— she's goin in. Now we don't do nothin but wait. I'll say somethin when somethin happens."

I rested the telephone on my shoulder and rolled down the window and threw my cigarette out. I had to turn on the key to roll down the window. They were electric.

Magda stirred in the corner. "Now?" she asked. "Is this when I get my briefing?"

"Now," I said. "The little blonde is from the same country as Van Zandt. Her father got run over in downtown Washington last week. Her father knew about Van Zandt's plans to get himself killed. It doesn't matter now how he found out. The little blonde's job is to go into the trade mission, and threaten to spill the whole mess. We're betting that they'll move her someplace where they can keep her out of sight and out of hearing. We're betting that they'll move her to the same place where they're holding my wife."

"Padillo," she said. "It's got all the nastiness of something he'd propose—using someone else's neck."

"If she doesn't come out in thirty minutes, we go in and get her."

"We?"

"The four of them and me. You can wait in the car."

"And if they move her, we follow them. Is that it?"

"That's it," I said.

"Then I go up to the door of wherever it is, knock politely, and when it's opened, I aim a gun at whoever opens it and tell him to open it all the way."

"I'll be with you," I said. "Our four friends will be close by."

"Then we go in, rescue your wife and Michael's little blonde thing and that's it. The curtain descends with me counting the final share of my payment."

"You've got it."

"Simple," she said. "Like everything he's ever done. Complicated, but simple, with someone bound to get hurt."

"Perhaps."

"We'll make a lovely couple going up to that door," she said. "How do you know they don't have orders to shoot all callers?"

"I don't. You can always shoot first."

"You sound awfully determined."

"It's my first wife."

She looked at me and smiled slightly. "Determined— even for a first wife."

"You did bring something to shoot with, didn't you?"

"Yes."

There wasn't much conversation after that. I lighted another cigarette and stared at the traffic. Magda curled in her corner of the big seat and tapped her fingers on her purse. After a while, she opened it, took out a compact and inspected her make-up. If she were going calling, she seemed to want to look nice.

"Hardman," the telephone said. "It's fifteen till and they comin out the front . . . Two and Missy . . . she between em . . . They all gettin in a car—Continental, dark blue . . . all three in the front seat . . . it's backin out . . . turnin onto Massachusetts and headin away . . ."

"Which way?" It was Padillo's voice.

"East . . . we're right behind em . . . You got it, Johnny ay?"

"Got it. We're comin."

"I'll take first tail," Hardman said. "Then we shift off nd you take it."

"O.K.," Johnny Jay said. "We rollin on Mass now."

"They comin your way, Mac."

"All right," I said. I started the car and pulled it up to ie corner, and pulled down the sun visor. The blue Con-nental sped by, Boggs at the wheel, Sylvia in the center,)arragh on the other side. They didn't seem to be doing uuch talking. The white pickup truck was about fifty feet ehind them, Tulip driving. I fell in behind the pickup.

"Where you at, Johnny Jay?" Hardman asked.

"Six blocks this side of the circle," he said.

"We're four blocks. I want you to take over at Dupont."

"I'm comin."

At Dupont Circle, the Continental turned down Nine-:enth. "He's turnin on Nineteenth, Johnny Jay. I'm going n to Connecticut."

"I got him in sight."

"You take the talkin then."

I followed the pickup truck as it turned right on Con-ecticut at Dupont Circle.

"This mother's movin," Johnny Jay said. "We're crossin 4 Street . . . goin straight . . . Now we're on K . . . turnin :ft on K . . . Red light at Eighteenth . . . Now we're goin .. Seventeenth . . . now Seventeenth and I . . . made the ght . . . now Pennsylvania and we made that one too . . . till on Seventeenth. . . ."

Johnny Jay kept talking as Boggs led him down Sev-nteenth to the Tidal Basin, up Main Avenue past what was left of Washington's waterfront, and then up M Street into the new southwest section of the city.

"I don't know where this mother's goin, but he's headin for home territory now," Johnny Jay said. "We at M and Van Streets now, baby."

"He goin past the Navy Yard?" Hardman asked.

"Look like he goin right past," Johnny Jay said.

"He hit that Navy Yard he can't turn right till he get to Eleventh. I'm goin to move up on him. You drop back."

"I'm droppin," Johnny Jay said.

We were moving down N Street in the southeast section as Hardman talked. At Half Street he turned left and then right on M. I was right behind the pickup and could see the Continental speeding down the double-laned boulevard on M that ran in front of the thirteen-block-long Navy Yard. At Eleventh Street, the Continental pulled over to the right lane, and turned right.

"He goin to Anacostia!" Hardman said. "Shit, man, nobody go there."

Anacostia was across the river from the rest of Washington and it might as well have been in the next country. There wasn't much to attract the tourist and the typical northwest Washington resident wasn't quite sure how to get there if he were ever unlucky enough to have cause to go. It was an area of quiet streets that were turning into a ghetto, but it would take another five years or so for that. At present, it was a mixture, perhaps thirty per cent white and seventy per cent Negro.

"Stick close, gentlemen," Hardman said, "cause I don't know this area too well."

"Who does?" Johnny Jay asked.

We crossed the Eleventh Street Bridge, and turned right. After that I got lost. We were in the briar patch. The

ontinental turned down a quiet residential street and I
rove slowly around the corner and stopped. The pickup
ollowed the Continental down half-a-block. The big white
uck with Nineball driving and Johnny Jay beside him
ith the phone in his hand turned the corner and pulled
up front of me.

I couldn't see the Continental. Hardman started talking
gain. "They parked in front of a house, two stories, brick,
d they goin in. Missy's between em. They knockin on
e door, somebody opening it, can't see who, and they've
ne gone in."

"They get ten minutes," I said.

"Can you see them, Mac?" It was Padillo's voice.

"No. The truck's blocking my view."

We waited. Magda stirred and opened her purse and
oked inside.

"The same two comin out now," Hardman said. "They
ttin in the car. They rollin it now."

"O.K.," I said. "The two of us will go up to the door;
u be on the sidewalk."

"Now?" Magda said.

"Now you start earning your money."

She looked through the window of the car at the cracked
ncrete sidewalk, the narrow houses that needed paint,
d the trees with the last of the year's leaves clinging as
they had been hung out to dry and forgotten.

"You know," she said as she pressed the handle of the
or, "I think I'm going to earn every cent."

— TWENTY-FOUR —

The house was built on a terrace but the grass had long since given up and disappeared. It was a fifteen-foot-wide rowhouse with a grey brick veneer. It had a window and a door on the first floor and two windows on the second. A porch with a shingled roof seemed to have been added to the front as an afterthought. Venetian blinds were lowered on the three windows.

I studied the houses next to it as Magda and I walked down the sidewalk. They were built from the same plans, but their windows were blank and staring. They were vacant. Some old newspapers were piled on their porches. A broken green tricycle with only one rear wheel rusted in the bare earth yard of the house on the right.

Concrete steps led from the sidewalk up the terrace. We took them, Magda going first, holding her purse with both hands. I looked back. Nineball and Johnny Jay were walking down the other side of the street making a show of looking at house numbers. Hardman and Tulip were doing the same thing on our side of the street, about thirty feet behind us.

We climbed the four steps to the porch. There was no bell, so I knocked on the door, standing to the right of Magda. There was no answer and I knocked again. Louder. The door opened about three inches.

"I beg your pardon," Magda said, "but I'm to pick up some furniture and I'm having trouble locating number 1537."

The door opened wider and a man's voice said: "This is 1523."

She took the gun out of her purse quickly and pointed it at him and said: "Open the door all the way and move back."

I reached for the screen door. But it was fastened. I had the revolver out of my coat pocket. "Unfasten the door," I said.

The man made no move to do so, and I had to open the screen door by jerking the hook and eye that held it shut out of its fastening. I got the screen open and hit the wooden door with my shoulder. I went through fast. A heavyset man in shirtsleeves with long brown hair was backing away from me, his right hand moving towards his right hip pocket. He was backing down a hall.

I waved my gun at him and said: "One more step and it goes off." He stopped. The hall ran to the rear of the house. To the left, along the wall, a flight of stairs led up to the second floor. To the right was what seemed to be the living room. Two men broke quickly out of it, both carrying guns.

"Watch your right," Magda snapped and shot one of the men in the stomach. He looked surprised and dropped his gun. It was an automatic. Then he sat down on the floor and held his stomach. The other man stopped and stood with his automatic in his hand, looking down at his friend on the floor.

"You shot him," he said, and there was a note of incredulity in his voice. Something flashed by my left side and I turned in time to see Hardman's big back with "Four-Square Movers" stitched across it in red thread going in low at the heavyset man with the long brown hair. The man had a gun out of his hip pocket by then and he tried to bring it down on Hardman's head, but the knife in the big Negro's right hand went into his side and the man screamed instead and dropped the gun.

Hardman got up and looked at the knife in his hand and shook his head slightly. Then he looked around as if for something to wipe it on and when he didn't find anything he knelt down and wiped it on the man's trousers. The man was moaning.

I turned to the one with the gun in his hand. He still held it, but it was pointed at the floor, dangling as if it were forgotten.

"Where are the two women?" I said.

"You shot him," the man said to Magda. "He was my friend." He had an accent like Darragh's and Boggs's. The man that Magda had shot lay on the floor and twitched. He was still holding his stomach, but he made no sound.

"Johnny Jay, you and Tulip get out on the porch and yell if you see somethin'," Hardman told them. They moved through the door.

"Where are the two women?" I said again.

"Upstairs," the man said. Nineball reached out and took the gun away from him. The man didn't seem to notice.

"Anyone else upstairs?" I said.

"No."

"I'll go with you," Magda said.

I nodded and started up the stairs. They were covered with a grey carpet that was worn through on the edge of the risers. The wallpaper was of impossibly pale roses with faded green stems and leaves. Only the thorns looked real.

I kept the revolver in my right hand as we went up. At the top, I turned right. There were three doors, one of them open and leading into a bathroom. I tried the second door; it opened into an empty bedroom. The third door was locked, but there was a key in it. I turned the key and pushed the door open wide and moved into the room quickly.

Sylvia Underhill sat in a chair between twin beds. She had a washcloth in her hand. She looked up, her eyes wide with fear and perhaps anger. Fredl lay on a bed, fully clothed except for her shoes. Her eyes were closed. She seemed asleep.

"Is she all right?" I asked.

"She's drugged," Sylvia said. "It's been awful and I got so frightened." She twisted the washcloth nervously in her hands. I moved to the bed and looked down at Fredl and put my hand on her forehead. It was too warm.

"I think she has fever," Sylvia said.

I put my revolver in the pocket of my topcoat and sat on the bed and held Fredl's wrist. I could feel her pulse and it was slow but steady enough. Her face was pale and her blond hair was spread out on the pillow.

"Are you all right?" I asked Sylvia.

"Yes," she said, but her voice didn't sound convincing.

"It's over now," I said.

"Not quite, McCorkle." It was Magda talking to me from across the room. I turned and looked at her. She stood by the door with the automatic in her hand. It looked like a Beretta. She held it steadily; there was no tremor in her hand.

"We're going to stay here for two more hours—you, me, your wife and Miss Underhill. You'll send the others away."

I just kept sitting on the bed. "You'll notice my gun is not aimed at you," she said. "It's aimed at your wife. If you try anything, I'll shoot her. And if you're still moving, I'll shoot you in the kneecap which is quite painful, but most effective."

"In two hours, Van Zandt will be dead, right?"

"Right."

"You teamed with Dymec," I said. I made it a statement, not an accusation.

"There was so much money involved."

"Why shoot the guy downstairs?"

"He didn't know who I was. Why should he?"

"Now what?"

"Now you walk carefully over to that door. Open it and call down to your friends. Tell them that you'll take care of your wife and the Underhill child. Tell them to leave and to take the unwounded man with them. And to keep him safe."

"Anything else?"

"If they ask about you, tell them that the girl and I are helping to dress your wife. We'll take her in the Cadillac when she's dressed."

I continued to sit on the bed.

"Move," she said. The automatic didn't waver. I got up and walked over to the door and opened it. Magda backed so that she had me in full view. I was in front of her, Fredl was to her left. Sylvia was to her left and slightly behind.

"Hardman," I called.

"Yo!"

"They're getting Fredl dressed."

"She O.K.?"

"She's O.K. You four take off. Take the guy that's not hurt with you. Leave the others. I'll meet you at Betty's. You got it?"

"What do you want me to do with him?"

"Keep him someplace safe."

"You need any help with Fredl?"

"No."

"We're leavin then."

Magda nodded. "Keep the door open," she said. "I want to hear them leave."

I kept it open until she could hear the front door downstairs close.

"Now you may go over and sit in the corner, McCorkle, like a good boy."

"Which corner?"

"The one just behind you. But first, you have a revolver in your coat pocket. I want you to take it out very slowly and put it on the floor."

"Gee, Magda, you think of everything," I said. I took the .38 out and put it on the floor.

"Now kick it gently towards me," she said.

I kicked it gently towards her.

"What happens after two hours? You just walk out into the street and call a taxi?"

"Something like that."

"I don't think so," I said. "I think in two hours you'll leave, all right, but the three of us will be dead. That's your assignment from Dymec, isn't it?"

"You have two entire hours to worry about it."

"How much was the payoff?"

"So much money, McCorkle. So very much lovely money."

"Enough to retire?"

"Quite enough."

"I always favored early retirement—especially after an active life."

"You chatter too much."

"I'm nervous."

Sylvia Underhill, slightly behind Magda, pulled up her skirt as if to adjust her hose. When her hands came up she held a nickel-plated .25 automatic in them. Her eyes were wide and she held the automatic with both hands, but it still shook. Her eyes asked me the question and I nodded my head just slightly and Sylvia Underhill shot Magda Shadid twice in the back. She held the small automatic in both hands and jerked the trigger. The first time, her eyes were closed. The second time she pulled the trigger, they were open. She looked as if she were going to cry.

Magda stumbled forward, caught herself and turned. "You little bitch," she said and tried to get her gun up so that she could shoot Sylvia Underhill or Fredl McCorkle. I don't think she cared which. I was across the room by then, the switchblade was open in my right hand, and it went into her back and the blade scraped her spine.

She fell then with the knife still in her back. I reached down and pulled it out and wiped it on the bedspread. Sylvia was crying. She sat in the chair, bent forward, the small automatic still in her hands, and cried.

"Let's go," I said.

She looked up at me. There was a lot of revulsion in her face. "I killed her," she said.

"I helped."

"I've never killed anything before, not even animals. Not even a bird."

I picked Fredl up from the bed. She didn't seem to weigh very much.

"Let's go," I said to Sylvia.

She rose, the automatic still dangling in her hand. "Put that in my pocket," I said. "The one on the floor, too."

She walked around the bed and picked up the .38 that I had kicked towards Magda and put it into my right coat pocket. She dropped hers into the other pocket where it clicked against the knife. I walked over to the door and turned. Sylvia was standing in the center of the room, staring down at the lifeless body.

"You'll have to open the door," I said. "I have my hands full."

"I didn't want to kill you," she said to the body on the floor.

— TWENTY-FIVE —

It was a long, difficult drive to Betty's. I went fast, unconscious of the speed limits, crossing the Anacostia River on the Eleventh Street Bridge and turning right on Potomac Avenue, I cut left on Pennsylvania Avenue and followed it to the Library of Congress, turned right on First Street, sped past the Supreme Court and the Senate Office Building, wound around the maze in front of Union Station, got on to North Capitol Street until I hit Florida Avenue, then caught Georgia Avenue at the old Griffith Stadium site and drove past Howard University until I came to Fairmont.

Sylvia Underhill held Fredl in her arms while I drove. Neither of us said anything. I tried the car's telephone once to see if the conference call was still working, but it was dead. I parked in the no parking zone in front of Betty's apartment house, went around the car, and helped Sylvia out. She needed help. A reaction seemed to have set in and she was trembling.

"Hold on a few more minutes," I said. I picked Fredl up and we walked up a flight of steps and into the building. I had Sylvia ring the doorbell. Betty answered it.

"Un-huh," she said. "Bring her into the bedroom. I'll get hold of Doctor Lambert. He's spectin to be called."

I didn't take off my shoes as I walked across the white carpet and into the room with the big oval bed. I put Fredl down on it gently.

"She's very pretty," Sylvia said from behind me.

"Yes, she is, isn't she."

Betty came into the bedroom. "She sick or hurt?"

"Doped."

She nodded as if it happened every day in her house. Maybe it did. "Doctor's on his way." She turned to Sylvia. "Who's this?"

"This is Sylvia. She helped us find my wife."

Betty looked at the girl carefully. "Looks like Sylvia needs a drink. She's shaking."

"So am I."

Betty put her hands on her hips. She was wearing lime green stretch pants, a white blouse, and no shoes. "You know where the liquor is. You all go on in the livingroom and I'll get your wife undressed and tucked into bed. Don't look like she's gonna be waking up anytime soon."

"Thanks," I said.

"And take off your shoes."

After I got my shoes off, I mixed two drinks and gave one to Sylvia. "Drink it," I said. "It'll help your shakes."

She nodded and drank. We sat in the livingroom until Doctor Lambert knocked on the door. He nodded at me. "Who's the patient?" he asked.

"My wife. She's in the bedroom."

He went in, carrying his doctor's bag, and I sat there

on the couch and stared at the white rug. Sylvia said not
ing. The doctor and Betty came out in a quarter of an hou

"I can't determine what they gave her," he said. "B
it was an injection—in her right arm. She's in no dange
but the best thing to do would be to let her sleep. I estima
she'll be out for another four or five hours at least."

"You sure she's all right?"

"Yes."

"Take a look at this one then," I said, nodding my he
at Sylvia.

"Has she been hurt?"

"In a way," I said. "But it's mostly fright. She does
like herself very much either."

The doctor's dark face was impassive. "Go take a lo
at your wife," he said. "I'll see what I can do for yo
friend."

I went back into the bedroom and looked down at t
oval bed where Fredl lay sleeping, the covers drawn
to her chin. She stirred slightly, but not much. I stood the
for what seemed to be a long time and looked at her a
I found myself smiling. I put my drink down on the dresse
then went back to the bed, bent down, and kissed Fre
on the forehead. She didn't stir. I stood there for a whi
longer, just looking at her and smiling until my jaws seem
to grow stiff, then I picked up the drink and went ba
into the livingroom.

Dr. Lambert was handing Sylvia a capsule and a gla
of water. "Some people," he said to me, "seem to thi
that liquor is the cure for everything."

I looked at the drink in my hand and then took a swallo
"I've known it to brighten a few dark moments," I sai

"It's a depressant," he snapped. "Not a stimulant."

"I didn't think she needed a pep pill."

"She needs to sleep," the doctor said testily, "not to brood. This will help her sleep."

"She can sleep on the couch," Betty said. "You want the floor?" she asked me.

"I have to go." I said.

"You don't look too well yourself," the doctor said. "You look beat."

"I'm all right," I said and waved my drink at him. "I'll stick to the home remedy."

"Liver," Doctor Lambert murmured. "It gets them all in the liver."

"What about the bill?" I said.

"Three hundred."

I got my billfold out and paid him. "I'll drop back by in a couple of hours," he said.

"Thanks."

He picked up his bag and moved to the door. "When's the last time you had a complete examination?" he said.

"Five or six years ago."

He shook his head. "A picture of health," he said. "Just yellowing at the corners."

"Thanks," I said.

He opened the door and said: "No charge." Then he was gone.

Betty went into the bedroom and returned with two pillows, some sheets and a blanket. She made up a bed on the couch, talking to herself as she worked. I went over and knelt on one knee by Sylvia. She was staring at her hands in her lap. "Get some sleep," I said. "You need it."

She looked up at me. "Are you leaving?"

"Yes."

"I'd like to see him—just once more."

"I'll tell him."

"I don't think I can sleep."

"Try."

She nodded. I rose and walked over to Betty. "Thank
for your help," I said.

She looked up at me and grinned. It was a wide, whit
grin with a lot of cynical sauciness in it. "You see Hard
man, you tell him he better get me a maid."

I smiled back at her. "I'll tell him."

"Come on, Sylvia," she said. "Let's get you to bed.'

I went over to the door and opened it. "They be a
right," Betty said. "I'll look after them both."

"Thanks," I said and left.

I parked Hardman's Cadillac on I Street and starte
walking the two blocks to the Roger Smith. It was tw
o'clock, three-quarters of an hour before Van Zandt's fou
car motorcade was supposed to turn down Pennsylvani
at the corner of Seventeenth. I found myself wonderin
how the old man liked taking a tour of Washington's sites
believing that he had only forty-five minutes to live.

I was approaching the corner of H and Eighteenth whe
a figure stepped out of a doorway and said: "You're late.
It was Padillo.

"I had a couple of things to do," I said. "It took longe
than I thought."

"There's a bar around the corner," he said. "You ca
tell me about them."

We walked around the corner and went into a bar tha
had a surplus of dark oak fixtures. The luncheon crow
was almost gone and a waitress gave us a booth in th
rear. I ordered a Scotch-and-water and Padillo said h
wanted a martini. When the drinks came and the waitres
left, Padillo said:

"We broke the conference call when Hardman said you were taking Fredl and Sylvia to Betty's."

"You broke it a little soon."

"How?"

"Sylvia had to help me kill Magda."

I told him about it then and he listened as he usually did, without showing much more surprise than if I had been telling him that the electronics stock I had touted to him had taken a turn for the worse.

"Where did Hardman take the other man—the third one?"

"I don't know."

"Is Fredl all right?"

"Yes."

"Sylvia?"

"Not too well. She wants to see you. One more time, she said."

He nodded and looked at his watch. "Now would be a good time to back out," he said.

"It would, wouldn't it?"

"It's not really our do anymore."

"No. Fredl's safe. Sylvia's all right."

"We can just walk back to the saloon," Padillo said. "Might even catch a cab."

"We could do that."

"Have a nice quiet lunch with a good bottle of wine."

"Read about it in the papers tomorrow."

Padillo looked at me. "But you won't."

"No."

"Why? Because some little girl with puppy-dog eyes saved your life?"

"Don't knock my excuses. I've got better ones than you do."

Padillo put a couple of bills on the table. "Let's go Mush is waiting in the lobby."

"Which way is Philip Price going to bounce?"

"I have no idea."

"What do we do?"

"Keep Dymec from shooting Van Zandt."

"How?"

"By persuasion."

"Will that work?"

"Let's find out."

We walked into the Roger Smith at two-twenty p.m. Mush was sitting in one of the chairs in the lobby, reading The Wall Street Journal through his dark glasses. He nodded his head twice as we walked into the elevator. He didn't seem to look at us.

I glanced around the lobby. There was no one else I knew. The elevator came and another man got in with us. He pressed the button for the third floor. When he got off Padillo pressed the tenth-floor button. "Mush has a description of Dymec and Price," Padillo said. "That now means that Dymec's gone up. Price hasn't shown yet."

We got off on the tenth floor and walked down to the thick door that said "Roof Garden." The door was painted a Chinese red and the lettering was in gold. We went through the door and stopped because of the two guns that were aimed at us.

One of the guns was an automatic. From where I stood it could have been a Colt Commander .38. I wasn't sure. But there was no mistaking the big fist that held it. That belonged to Hardman. The other gun, a revolver, was in the hand of Philip Price and he seemed to know what he was doing. We let the door close behind us.

"Roof garden's done closed," Hardman said. "For the season."

Padillo looked at me. "Your friend," he said.

"He was on our side this morning."

We were standing in the small landing that faced the stairs which led to the roof. Hardman and Price were up five or six steps, aiming their guns at us in a calm, professional manner. Their advantage of height didn't hurt any.

"Just stand easy," Price said. "Keep your hands in front of you and don't ask if you can light a cigarette."

"I don't get it, Hardman," I said.

"Money, baby. Fifty thousand is a lot of money."

"We decided to consolidate," Price said. "In return for your complete cooperation, your African friends agreed to raise the fee. Enormously."

"They went way up," Hardman said. "I just couldn't say no." He sounded almost apologetic.

Price glanced at his watch. "It shouldn't be long now."

"That little brunette gal with the pistol was supposed to hold you, Mac," Hardman said. "What happened?"

"I killed her."

He nodded. "That's more for us," he said to Price.

"So it is," Price said.

"Your wife all right?" Hardman said.

"She's all right."

"I like Fredl," Hardman said. "Didn't want nothin to happen to her."

"It didn't."

"What happened to you, Price?" Padillo said. "I thought you were going for the letter."

"I don't need the letter," he said.

"Just money."

Price smiled. "There seems to be enough for all."

Padillo turned slowly and leaned against the wall. He kept his hands in sight. "Your friend Hardman ever try to beat a murder rap?"

"You'll have to ask him," I said.

"How about it, Hardman?" Padillo said.

"We're comin out of this one nice and clean. Ain't gonna be no mess."

"Then you fixed it with Mush?" Padillo said.

"Mush works for me, baby."

Padillo turned his head to look at Hardman. "What did you send Mush up to Baltimore for? Heroin?"

"I don't fool with H. Mush was goin after acid. Five hundred grams of lysergic acid diethylamide."

"That's a lot of LSD," Padillo said. "What's the market? I thought you could mix up a batch in the bathroom sink."

"Gettin tough, baby. Feds are crackin down and so're the states. That much acid is good for a little less'n five million trips at five bucks per retail. I figure to wholesale it at thirty cents a trip."

"The Englishman was supposed to have it?"

"He supposed to."

"But they shoved him into the freezer. You think the acid went with him?"

"I don't know, baby."

"Let me ask you something else, Hardman. How did Mush know who I was?"

"Didn't. He just found Mac's address in your pocket."

"You're talking too much, Padillo," Price said.

"You're in the business, Price. Do you think I'd carry a piece of paper around in my pocket with an address on it?"

"Not bloody likely. But shut up anyway."

"If I didn't have any address in my pocket, Hardman, then how did Mush know about McCorkle and me?"

"You ain't making sense," Hardman said.

"You're smarter than that, Hardman," I said. "Even I can figure it out."

"How long's Mush been workin for you?" Padillo said.

The big man took one step down the stairs. "You saying Mush is a ringer?"

"You didn't get your acid, did you?" Padillo said. "You got me instead. Why?"

"Mush get my acid?"

"Shut up," Price said. "We're going to have to leave here in a few minutes. You can worry about it then."

"Man's talking about maybe a million dollars' worth of acid—wholesale," Hardman said. "I wanna know what happened. I gotta find out. Mush get my acid?" he demanded of Padillo.

"No," Padillo said.

"Who got it?"

"The United States Treasury."

— TWENTY-SIX —

The door from the hall slammed open and Mush came through it, moving fast. Padillo seemed to have expected him because he lunged for the steps and jerked Price's legs out from under him. Hardman kicked at Mush's head, but missed, and Mush scrambled on up the stairs. I grabbed Hardman's other leg and gave it a yank and he fell backwards and the gun clattered down the steps. Price was up and moving quickly up towards the roof, Padillo behind him. Hardman wasn't down for more than a second. He moved too fast for a man of his size. I couldn't move like that and Hardman carried fifteen more pounds than I did.

I was still at the bottom of the stairs and Hardman was on the sixth step. He pulled a knife from his pocket and flicked it open. Price and Padillo disappeared around a corner at the top of the stairs. Mush was no longer in sight.

"You ain't goin nowheres, Mac. You stayin here with me."

"I'm going up the stairs," I said.

"You ain't goin by me."

"You're still clean on this one, Hardman. You can move out. I'll let you by."

He laughed. "You a gentleman, ain't you? You gonna let me by. Shit, you somethin, baby."

"Go on, Hardman. You've got time."

"I ain't goin nowheres and you ain't goin nowheres."

"I'm going up the stairs," I said.

"Not past me."

I reached into my coat pockets and took out the knife with my left hand and the .38 with my right. "You're wrong about two things. One, I'm no gentleman. If I were a gentleman, I'd try to take you with the knife. Now the gun says I go past you." I pointed it in his general direction.

"No gun, Mac. Gun'll bring the law."

"This place is soundproofed," I said. "It keeps the band noise down."

"You won't shoot me," he said.

"You talk a lot."

Hardman started down the steps toward me. He held the knife in his right hand, his arm up and out a little. The blade was flat with the floor, the easier to pass through the ribs, I suppose. He came down two full steps. "Gimme your gun, Mac."

I shook my head. "Go on out the door and you're home free."

"You ain't gonna shoot, Mac." He took one more step. He moved slowly, but with curious grace.

"I'm going past you, Hardman."

"No," he said. He grinned. He took another step and he was still grinning when I shot him. Then the grin disappeared, and he tried one more step. I shot him again.

He said, "Shit, man," and fell the last step and sprawled in the corner and lay still.

I went up the stairs three at a time. Padillo and Price were in the anteroom that led to the roof. Price was in front of the stall where you checked your coats. He had lost his gun on the stairs, but he had a knife out. It seemed to be the day for knives. Padillo's back was to me as Price moved towards him slowly. Price kept his eyes on Padillo's right hand which also had a knife in it.

"If you move over, I'll shoot him," I said.

"I'll drop flat on the floor, and then you can shoot him," Padillo said.

I pointed the gun at Price. "When he drops flat on the floor, I'll shoot you," I told him. "I've got four rounds left. I should be able to hit you with one."

"I don't think he wants to be shot," Padillo said and straightened up and put away his knife. Price looked at the one he held in his hand, shrugged, and tossed it on the floor.

Padillo jerked his head towards the French doors at the top of the stairs that opened onto the roof. "Move over there, Price."

"All right," the man said.

"Keep your gun on him," Padillo said and moved quickly over to the doors. I motioned Price towards them. Through the doors' glass we could see a strange dance on the polished marble floor. Dymec and Mush were locked together as each struggled to get a killing hold. They seemed to glide around the dance floor. The rifle lay near its edge. The two men broke apart and Mush tried to produce a revolver from his coat pocket. Its hammer snagged on his lining and Dymec kicked it as if he were kicking a soccer ball and the gun flew out of Mush's hand and landed a dozen feet away.

Dymec reached behind his neck and produced a thin-bladed knife.

"Make him come to you," Padillo said softly.

"Who's getting the advice?" I asked.

"Mush."

Dymec came at him. The Negro jumped back slightly and Dymec's concrete-colored face took on an earnest, thoughtful look. He turned slowly as Mush moved around him. Then he feinted and Mush tried for the right arm, but missed, and Dymec's knife went through his coat and into his side. Mush looked surprised and knelt on the floor and opened his coat to look at what caused him to hurt so bad.

Dymec picked up the rifle and ran quickly to the east edge of the building, glancing at his watch as he ran.

"I thought Mush could take him," Padillo said.

I looked at my watch. It was forty minutes after two. "That leaves it up to us."

"No," Padillo said. "Just me."

Dymec checked his rifle and aimed it between the posts of the chest-high railing. It made a comfortable rest. Padillo ran across the dance floor. Dymec heard him. He tried to get the rifle from between the posts, but Padillo hit him in the side with both feet. The rifle fell to the floor and Dymec was down on his hands and knees. He looked up at Padillo, said something, and jumped at him, his left hand out and stiff and extended. Padillo caught the hand, twisted and tried to throw Dymec, but the grey-faced man seemed to have anticipated it and drove his right hand hard into Padillo's left side. Padillo went white and started to bend over and Dymec aimed a kick at his head, but Padillo caught the foot and threw it upwards and Dymec fell. He fell hard, striking his head on the edge of the concrete railing. He lay still and his head was cocked at an odd angle. Padillo bent over Dymec and produced a cream-colored envelope from his jacket pocket. Then he straightened up and motioned to me.

Mush was still on his knees in the middle of the danc floor and I herded Price towards him. Padillo was kneelin, by Mush when we got there.

"How do you feel?"

"It's not bad," Mush said. "You stopped him?" Hi southern accent was gone.

"Yes. You're Treasury, aren't you?"

Mush nodded, his face screwed up in pain. "Narcotic Bureau."

"How'd you make me in Baltimore?"

"There were just two of you supposed to be on tha boat. They gave me a print-out on both of you. You weren' five-foot, three-inches tall and fifty years old."

"They thought I might have the acid?"

"One of you did."

"What are you going to do with it?" Padillo said.

Mush grimaced again. "You saw it?"

Padillo nodded. "Those two who jumped you. One o them was carrying something. He dropped it. It must hav been something you wanted."

"You'll have to teach me that Juarez judo again. I didn' seem to learn too well."

"You didn't turn it in, did you?"

"The acid?"

"That's right."

Mush stared at Padillo. "Not yet. You want a cut?"

"Hardman said it would make a million dollars' worth of sugar cubes."

"He was low."

"And that's why there aren't any Federal cops up here."

"That's why," Mush said.

"O.K.," Padillo said. "Now you're a rich man and a hero, too. You keep the acid."

Mush opened his mouth wide and squeezed his eyes shut. The cut seemed to hurt. "I'm not keeping it," he said. "I thought about it, but—" He shrugged and even the shrug hurt.

"One thing," Padillo said. "Are you really a Muslim?"

"Maybe," Mush said. "That acid would finance a hell of a lot of trips."

"What kind?" Padillo said.

"To Mecca."

"But you're going to turn it in?"

Mush nodded. "I'm going to turn it in."

"O.K. You won't be a rich man, but you'll be a hero. Your story is that you found out about the assassination attempt through Hardman at the last moment. Then you shot him and took care of Dymec. McCorkle and I weren't even near the place. Price helped you. All right?"

Mush tried to stand and Padillo helped him up. "If I told it any differently, they'd start asking questions. I haven't got much choice, have I?"

"Not much," Padillo said. "Some perhaps, but not enough to bother with."

"How about him?" Mush said, nodding towards Price.

"He'll be a hero, too, but quietly."

I took the .38 out of my pocket and put it in Mush's hand. "This is what you shot Hardman with."

Mush looked down at the revolver. "I liked Hardman," he said. Then he looked at his watch. "The man's about due."

"Can you make it over to look?" Padillo said.

"It's not that bad," Mush said.

I helped Mush over to the east edge of the building.

We looked down to the corner of Seventeenth and Pennsylvania. Traffic was light and the bright October sun mad
the Executive Office Building look a little less like an ol
grey ogre. On a new building at the southwest corner o
the intersection, two men practiced putting on a roof-to
green. Van Zandt's party was only three minutes late. Tw
motorcycle policemen turned the corner at Seventeenth o
to Pennsylvania. Behind them was a closed, black lim
ousine followed by an open car with three men sitting i
the rear seat. No crowds lined the sidewalk, although
few people stopped to glance at the procession. Two othe
black cars followed the open convertible. Two mor
motorcycle policemen brought up the rear.

We stared down at the small parade. "Right about no
would be perfect," Padillo said.

"Not much wind," Price agreed.

Mush said something in Arabic.

"What was that?" I said.

"From the Koran again," Padillo said. "'Wheresoeve
you be, death will overtake you, although you be in loft
towers.'"

I could see Van Zandt clearly now, even from eleven sto
ries up. Darragh was next to him. I didn't recognize the ma
on the other side. Boggs was driving. Van Zandt wore n
hat and his long white hair floated around his head in th
breeze created by the open car. He turned his face up to th
building where we stood. The car slowed. I waved at him
Darragh was looking up now and I waved at him, too.

Neither of them waved back.

— TWENTY-SEVEN —

We left Mush to take credit for spoiling the assassination and brought Price with us to the parking lot where we got Hardman's Cadillac out.

"Which way?" I said.

"Where does the British Resident live, Price?"

"That's not part of it," he said.

"It is now."

"You'll ruin it."

"Not when he sees the letter."

"I'll get the letter to him."

"I'd feel better if I did it."

"You don't seem to trust Price," I said.

"Do you?"

"Not in the least."

"Where's your Resident?"

Price sighed. "He lives near American University." He recited an address.

"Will he be home?"

"He's always home. He's writing a book. He's an historian."

I drove to the address that Price gave us. It was a quiet tree-shaded street with large, middle-aged houses set well back from the street. Two mothers pushed strollers filled with plump children down the sidewalk in the mild afternoon air. The number Price gave us was a white frame house that had two stories, a wraparound porch, and an indeterminate architectural style. I suppose it could have been called comfortable. Parking was no problem in that neighborhood and I pulled the car up to the curb next to a large tidy pile of autumn leaves. The yard in front of the house had a lot of shrubbery and flower beds and its occupant seemed to have spent time taking care of things.

We walked up to the house, climbed the four steps of the porch, and rang the bell. A man opened the door.

"Well," he said when he saw Price. Then he repeated it: "Well."

"I couldn't help it," Price said.

The man nodded. He was about fifty and wore a grey woolen sweater that buttoned up the front, dark grey slacks and a pair of silver-rimmed glasses that covered mild eyes that were almost the color of his sweater. He was also a little fat.

"Well," he said for the third time. "Perhaps you should come in." He didn't seem overly concerned about whether we did or not.

He held open the screen door and Price went in first followed by Padillo and me. When we turned around, the man was holding a gun. It wasn't aimed at us; it was just held so that we could see it.

"I don't suppose this will be necessary," he said and moved the gun a little.

"No," Price said.

"Then I shall put it away." He walked over to a small table that held a lamp, opened a drawer, and put the gun in it. He turned to us again.

"Perhaps you should introduce your friends," he said to Price.

"Padillo and McCorkle," Price said. He didn't bother to tell us who the man in the sweater was. The mild eyes behind the glasses widened slightly when Padillo's name was mentioned.

"Well," the man said, "do sit down."

We were standing in the livingroom which was filled with chairs and sofas and the usual bric-a-brac. A fire burned in the fireplace at one end of the room. Padillo and I sat in two easy chairs; Price and his employer, I suppose, sat side by side on a couch.

"Michael Padillo," the man in the sweater said.

"I'm in your book," Padillo said. "I want out."

"Yes," the man said and reached into his sweater pocket and pulled out a pipe. He didn't need it really. He had the worn sweater and the comfortable house and the burning fireplace. He didn't need the pipe to complete the scene. We waited while he filled it and lighted it and put his wooden matches in an ashtray.

"In my book, you say."

"Stan Burmser told me about it," Padillo said. "You know Stan?"

"Hmmm."

"Stan said you gave it to Price and I know you gave it to Price because he tried the other night and missed. Didn't you, Price?"

Price didn't say anything. He looked at the carpet.

"How did Burmser know?" the man said.

"He's doubled one of your people. He didn't say whic
one."

"Interesting."

"I've got a trade for you. This for getting out of you
book." Padillo produced the cream-colored envelope an
handed it to me. "I want McCorkle to read it first."

I read it. The letter was signed by Van Zandt and wi
nessed by Boggs and Darragh. It had an official-lookin
red wax seal on it. It said that certain persons had bee
engaged to "effect my assassination" and that "this wa
done to create a proper climate for understanding the prob
lems that confront my country." There was more to it, b
those were the key phrases. I handed the letter to the ma
in the sweater.

He read it and the kindly, professorial manner almo
vanished.

"Is it real?" he demanded.

"It's real," Padillo said.

"When was the attempt to be made?"

Padillo looked at his watch. "A half-hour or so ago."

Padillo told him what had happened. "When it come
out, though, it comes out this way: The plot was foiled—
that's a good word, isn't it?—by the British Secret Servic
or MI 6 or whatever you want to use, aided by Mustaph
Ali, a member of the Black Muslims."

"Come off it, Padillo," Price said.

"That's the way it comes out," Padillo said.

The man in the sweater tapped the cream-colored lett
on the coffee table in front of him and looked at Padill
"All right. It's a trade."

"What happens next?"

"We'll give our Ambassador to the UN time enough t
draft a speech. When is the old man due in New York?

"Tomorrow," Price said.

"Will he go?"

"He knows that someone now has that letter."

"Does he know who?"

"No."

The man in the sweater took off his glasses and polished them on his sleeve. "Well," he said again. "There's much to be done." He rose. The rest of us rose too. "I think you'd better remain here, Price," the man said.

He walked with us to the door. "You're no longer working for Burmser, Mr. Padillo?"

"No."

"Have you considered other employment?"

"No."

"Would you be interested?"

"I don't think so," Padillo said. "I'm retired."

"If you change your mind, please let me know," the man said. "We perhaps don't pay as well, but—"

"I'll keep it in mind," Padillo said.

"Do," the man said.

We went through the door and out into the afternoon air. The man in the grey sweater watched us from behind his screen door. He stood there and tapped the cream-colored letter against his left thumb until I opened the car door and got in.

"I have to meet my wife," I said to Padillo.

He looked at me and grinned. "Think she'll be on time?"

The next time I saw Michael Padillo was three days later. He was standing at the bar listening to the lameduck congressman. The Congressman had a large pile of money next to his drink. "Strictly cash from now on," he was telling Padillo. "Credit cards are an inflationary danger."

"A threat to the economy," Padillo said, excused him self, and walked over to me.

"Fredl's joining us for dinner," I said.

"Good. How is she?"

"She's all right."

"Still angry?"

"She's about over it."

"It was a tough story to have to sit on."

The story about the assassination attempt had made splash and Fredl had fumed as she read it and watched unfold on television. Great Britain's Ambassador to th United Nations had made a rouser of a speech, waving th letter in evidence. Van Zandt had fled back to his countr and his cabinet had resigned. There was some more tal about economic sanctions. Mush was something of a cu riosity in the press for a few days and his cover as narcotics agent was broken. He resigned several days late the papers said, "to devote his full time to the Black Mus lim cause." The British Secret Service received a discree pat on the back and a few editorials wondered how th FBI had been keeping itself busy. Near the end of the thir day, the story was dying.

Padillo and I went over to the bar and Karl moved dow to serve us.

"The Congressman's back, I see."

"He's thinking of running again next term," Karl said "I discouraged him."

"I'll try a vodka martini," I said. Padillo said he woul too. Karl mixed the drinks and served them. "Congres adjourned today," he said.

"That'll leave your mornings free."

"You can go back and read about the eighty-nine or s

at you didn't have the chance to hang around," Padillo
id.

Karl shook his head gloomily. "It's not the same," he
id and moved on down the bar to a customer.

Padillo shifted his drink around on the bar, making the
ttern of a small oblong box.

"They came back. Not Burmser; it was a new pair. New
me anyway."

I looked into the mirror. There was nothing to say yet.

"Sylvia said to say goodbye," he said.

"I thought she might stay."

He picked up his drink and inspected it. "That was
entioned."

"But you discouraged it."

"Yes."

"When did they come back? The pair, I mean."

"This afternoon. I've been restored to the good-graces
tegory."

"What about you and Sylvia?"

"We talked."

"About what; your yellow shadow?"

"That was mentioned."

"Some days you talk too much."

Padillo sighed and tasted his drink. "Some days I think
u're right." He paused and looked into the mirror. "I
ay not be around for a few weeks."

I nodded. "Where'll you be?"

He almost smiled, but didn't quite make it. "I think
meone's looking for her husband." I turned and Fredl
d just come through the door. She paused and glanced
ound and when she saw me, she smiled. There were a
eat many things I would do for that smile.

"Where're you going to be?" I said again.

Padillo sipped his drink. "Out of town," he said.

I left the bar and Padillo and walked quickly toward Fredl. I didn't bother to notice the color of his shadow.

Return to Mark